P9-EGD-632

DEC 1989

1295

W
Con

Conley, Robert J.
   The saga of Henry Starr / Robert J.
Conley. -- New York : Doubleday, c1989.
   177 p. ; 22 cm.
   ISBN 0-385-23957-2

   1. Starr, Henry, 1873-1921--Fiction.
2. Cherokee Indians--Fiction. I. Title

20 NOV 89   19723386 RSVAme   89-33801

The Saga of Henry Starr

The Saga of
Henry Starr

ROBERT J. CONLEY

A DOUBLE D WESTERN
Doubleday
NEW YORK   LONDON   TORONTO   SYDNEY   AUCKLAND

A Double D Western Book
Published by Doubleday, a division of
Bantam Doubleday Dell Publishing Group, Inc.
666 Fifth Avenue, New York, New York 10103

Double D, Doubleday,
and the portrayal of the two D's
are trademarks of Doubleday, a division of
Bantam Doubleday Dell Publishing Group, Inc.

Library of Congress Cataloging-in-Publication Data applied for.

ISBN 0-385-23957-2
Printed in the United States of America
August 1989
First Edition
OG

For Dave West and Frank Breneisen

AUTHOR'S NOTE

The Saga of Henry Starr is a novel. It is, however, based on the actual life of Henry Starr. In fact, Henry Starr's own book, *Thrilling Events,* was a primary source for this narrative. In *The Saga of Henry Starr,* where controversy exists (as in the disappearance of Kid Wilson), I have simply taken a position—one that suits my purposes as a novelist. I have taken other liberties, leaving out certain historical personages, renaming others. These kinds of choices are, after all, part of the selection process that is a major prerogative of writers of fiction.

The Saga of Henry Starr

The young cowboy rode hard, lashing at the big sorrel mare to urge her on. They splashed through freshets and churned up the soggy prairie ground, but in spite of his efforts, he arrived at the swollen stream too late to help. The others there before him had already managed to urge the last frightened cow back across through the swift, cold water to the proper side. He saw the cold, wet cows, smelled their wet hair, and heard them bawling against the background noise of the roaring water and the cursing of the cowboys. He pulled his panting, sweating mount to a halt in the midst of the other cowboys and had no more than dismounted when he felt himself jerked forward and off-balance by the big, burly hands of Clint Chambers.

"Damn you, Starr," said the big man, "that's my horse you're riding."

Henry Starr wrenched Chambers' hands loose from his shirtfront and backed off a couple of steps, slipping in the wet ground and regaining his balance. He tried to think of an appropriate response, but Chambers didn't give him time to formulate it.

"You damn near rode him to death," Chambers continued. "Look at him."

"Mr. Roberts told me to get down here quick," said Henry. "When the boss says to move fast, I move, and I don't care whose horse I kill."

"Yeah, well, I notice that you didn't get down here quick enough to do any work," said Chambers, giving Henry a rough shove, "you damned lazy redskin."

Henry felt the anger suddenly boil up inside him even as he staggered backward from the shove, again sliding in the mud beneath his feet. He was embarrassed. The others were watching. As Henry caught his balance and doubled up his fists to retaliate, a third cowboy stepped in front of him, grabbing him by the shoulders.

"Hold on, Henry," he said.

"I didn't start this," said Henry. "He did."

Two others took hold of Chambers' arms and held him back.

"Turn me loose," shouted the big man. "By God, I'll teach him a lesson."

"Just calm down," said the cowboy who was holding Henry. "We still got work to do. If you two got a grudge, settle it later. Come on. Mount up." Henry shrugged and turned toward the horse he had ridden up on.

"No you don't," said Chambers. "Not on my horse."

"Suit yourself," said Henry, and he turned away from Chambers' horse. Chambers climbed quickly into the saddle and started riding toward the ranch house. Henry thought that for a man who had just wanted to fight him for having ridden his horse too hard, Chambers was sure moving out fast. *The hypocrite*, he thought.

"Here," said the calm cowboy, handing Henry the reins to another mount. "This is the one he rode out on."

"Thanks."

All during the ride back to the ranch house, Henry seethed. He was burning inside. He was seventeen years old and full of the pride of youth, and he was an Indian working in the midst of a crew of white men. He had been pushed and yelled at in front of other men. He had been made to look foolish, slipping and sliding in the mud. He had been chastised for having done something he felt he had every right to do—more than that, something that he was, in fact, obligated by his employer to do. The back of his neck burned from the humiliation. He had left home because his white stepfather treated him, he felt—no, he was certain—unfairly—treated him like a snot-nosed kid with no sense and no rights. He could recall the many times C.N. had told him over and again to wash his neck even though he had just done so. C.N. thought that his brown skin was dirty. Well, he had gone out on his own, and he would not be treated that way again. He did miss his mother, but then, well, she just shouldn't have married that white trash, C. N. Walker.

Back at the ranch house, Henry went inside to talk to the boss. He found Roberts in his office, sitting behind the big desk.

"You get those cows turned back, Henry?"

"Yeah," said Henry, shuffling his feet and looking down at the floor and suddenly wishing that he had done a better job of cleaning the mud off his boots before coming in to see the boss. "Well, really, the other boys had it done by the time I got there, but that's not what I came to talk about."

Roberts looked up from his paperwork.

"What is it, Henry?" he said.

"I'm quitting."

"You're quitting? What for? Haven't I been fair to you?"

"You've been more than fair, Mr. Roberts. I've got nothing against you."

"Then what is it?"

Henry told Roberts about the incident with Chambers and his horse. Roberts took a deep breath and leaned back in his big office chair with a creak. He nodded knowingly.

"I already heard about that," he said. "Chambers beat you in here and told me all about it. His side of the story, of course. I'll tell you what I told him. He was wrong. You were in the right. When a man hires on with me, he hires on his horse, too. I sent you to do a job, and that horse was available. You don't have to quit on account of that."

"Thanks, Mr. Roberts," said Henry, "but I guess I'll be moving on anyhow."

"I wish you wouldn't."

Henry just looked at the floor, so Roberts reached into a drawer of the desk and pulled out a cashbox. He counted out some money onto the desk.

"You've been a good hand," he said, "but if you've made up your mind, I won't try to change it for you. Here's what I owe you."

Henry took the money and shoved it into his pocket.

"Thanks, Mr. Roberts," he said.

"If you ever want a job back here again," said Roberts, "it's yours. And if you need a reference from me for a job somewhere else, I'll give you a damn good one. You tell them that."

"I appreciate that," said Henry. "Be seeing you."

He turned and walked out of the house and soon found himself riding aimlessly across the prairie. He was fantasizing a finish to the argument with Chambers—one in which he thrashed the bully with his fists. Gradually the anger subsided, and Henry began to marvel at the extent of the open prairie. He was still in the Cherokee Nation (though people were beginning to refer to it collectively with its neighboring Nations as "Indian Territory"), but he was as far north as he had ever been in his short life. He had spent nearly all of his seventeen years in the thickly wooded hill country around Fort Gibson. Henry's memories of Fort Gibson were emotionally mixed. The earliest remembrances, from the days when his father, George, known as "Hop," was still alive, were pleasant, but they had been far too few. Henry's mother had remarried after the death of Hop Starr, and Henry's new stepfather was C. N. Walker, a white man. Henry hadn't liked C.N. from the beginning, and when C.N. had sold Henry's horse and saddle, bought and paid for with Henry's own money, money he had earned for himself,

the young man had left home for good. He had wandered
north, an incredible eighty-some-odd miles away from
home, and found a job on the Roberts Ranch.

Roberts, too, was a white man, Henry mused. Things
were quickly changing in the Cherokee Nation. He could
remember a time when whites had been few and far between, but the Nation's government had allowed more
and more renters to move in, and white men married
Cherokee women for land rights in the Cherokee Nation.
In addition, droves of whites had simply wandered into
the Nation and squatted. Roberts was decent enough, but
it seemed to Henry that C. N. Walker and Clint Chambers
were more representative of the race. He longed for the
good old days, which, of course, were not much more
than ten years behind him, and then an ironic realization
surfaced in his brain.

He had thought that he was riding aimlessly across the
prairie, but, in fact, his path was leading directly to the
home of the Morrisons—Mr. and Mrs. Morrison and their
daughter, Mae. The Morrisons were renters. Mae was
Henry's sweetheart. He was feeling bad, and he wanted to
see her, and they were white.

2

Pretty, young Mae Morrison was in the yard outside her parents' rented cabin, turning the crank at the well to draw up a bucket of water. She was barefoot, and the flour-sack dress she wore clung to her sweating flesh. Her brown hair was blowing in the wind. Some errant strands stuck to her face. She turned the crank almost with ease. She was not a frail girl. Her skin was tanned—almost, Henry Starr thought as he rode up into the yard, as dark as his own. As the horse and rider approached, kicking up puffs of dust from the flat prairie, dry already under the hot sun in spite of the recent heavy rains, Mae looked up and recognized Henry. She hauled the bucket on up out of the well and unhooked it from the rope.

"Henry," she said, her voice betraying a certain amount of surprise, "what are you doing here?"

Henry dismounted and let the reins trail in the dust. He noticed a few puddles of water standing around here and there, witnesses to the heavy rains in an otherwise dry setting. He took a step or two toward Mae, his thumbs hooked in the waistband of his trousers, his head ducked, eyes on the toes of his well-worn boots. He didn't know what he was doing there, but he didn't really want to tell her that. He was there because he was drawn to her. He had never had a sweetheart before. And she was a lovely one, he thought. He was there because he really had no other place to go. He was there because he had found himself traveling in that direction without having given it any particular thought.

"Oh," he said, "I just thought I'd stop by and see if there's anything I could give you a hand with."

Mae brushed some of the wild strands of hair away from her face with one hand, her other hand holding the bucket of water at arm's length. Water dripped from the bucket, forming a small but spreading patch of mud at her feet. Her toes dug into the mud. The picture was not, Henry realized, what most folks would think of as especially ladylike and dainty, but to Henry it was beautiful. It was real. Mae belonged to the land, he thought. She fit her setting the way—well, the way Henry fit his saddle.

"No," she said, "I mean, why aren't you at work?"

Henry walked boldly to Mae and put his arms around her, pulling her toward him. As he started to kiss her, she turned her face away from his, and he kissed her cheek, tasting the salty perspiration. He savored the taste. It was the taste of Mae.

"Henry," she said, "shouldn't you be at work?"

Henry let go of Mae and reached for the water bucket, pulling it out of her grip.

"Here," he said, "let me tote this bucket for you."

"Will you answer my question?"

Henry turned his back on Mae and started walking toward the house.

"I quit that job," he said.

After Henry had taken the water into the house, a small log cabin, and had said hello to Mrs. Morrison, he and Mae walked out back and strolled between the rows of corn in the garden. The rains had not yet had a noticeable effect on the scrawny corn that Mr. Morrison was trying to raise. The stalks were only as high as Henry's shoulders, and the husks had a sad, dry look. Henry held Mae's hand in his. Their palms were both sweaty. He told her the story of Clint Chambers' horse, and he told her how Mr. Roberts had not wanted him to quit. He told the whole story, being careful not to leave out any details, including how it all had made him feel.

"But I quit anyway," he said. "I just didn't want to be around those people anymore."

They walked on some more in silence. As they came to the end of a corn row and rounded it to stroll down another, Mae broke the silence.

"What will you do now?" she asked. "Go home?"

Henry stopped walking. He turned loose of Mae's hand and began to fumble with some drying corn tassels that were blowing in the wind with a rattling sound on a stalk there beside him.

"I don't have a home," he said.

"I mean your mother's house," said Mae.

It was a few seconds before Henry answered.

"When she married C.N.," he said, "that place stopped being my home. She chose him. I didn't. And I don't have to live with him. I guess there might be a good stepfather somewhere, but I haven't seen him. And if there is one, C. N. Walker is sure not it. He just married my mother for what he could get out of us."

Henry thought bitterly about his horse and saddle.

"No," he said. "I'm not going back there."

"What will you do then?" said Mae.

"Oh, I don't know," said Henry. "I guess something will turn up. Don't worry about it. Okay?"

It was Mae's turn to pause and think. She ambled along a few steps ahead of Henry, brushing the rough cornstalks with her hand. When she stopped and turned around to face him, she dug her bare feet into the dusty earth as if they were seeking moisture below the dry top layer of dirt. She looked at Henry, then reaching down the front of her homemade dress, she pulled out a string that was hanging around her neck. There was something on the end of the string, which she held tightly in her fist.

She gave a sharp tug, breaking the string, then held the fist out toward Henry.

"I have something for you," she said.

Henry walked toward her as she opened the fist to reveal a gold ring.

"Will you wear it for me?"

Henry took the ring from her sweaty palm and tried it on. It fit the little finger on his right hand.

"Yes," he said. "I'll wear it. Always."

Once again he reached out to take her in his arms, and this time, when he leaned forward to kiss her lips, she did not turn her face away. He was no longer thinking about Clint Chambers and his horse, about the humiliation of the confrontation in front of the other cowboys, about the loss of his job or about C. N. Walker. Mae felt good in his arms. Her lips felt good pressing onto his. He thought of nothing else. He felt just fine.

Henry had been right not to worry about the job. It was only a few days later that he found himself sitting idly on a street in Nowata, a small town not far from the Roberts Ranch. He had found a chair on the wooden sidewalk of the main street of town, and he sat down in it to rest up from his footloose wandering and began whittling on a stick with his pocketknife. He had just gotten a fine, sharp point on the stick when a wagon drew up in the street there before him. The driver hauled back on the reins and set the brake as the dust rose around him. His clothes indicated to Henry that he was a prosperous man, and he appeared to be in his early thirties.

"Morning," he said.

Henry looked up and saw that the man was talking to him.

"Howdy," he said.

"You're Henry Starr, ain't you?" asked the driver.

"Yeah."

"Well, my name's Charles Todd. I've got a little ranch out here. I heard you quit Roberts. That right?"

"That's right," said Henry. He quit whittling and looked at the man.

"You looking for a job?" asked Todd.

"Well, sir," said Henry, pitching the stick aside and folding up his pocketknife, "I just might be."

And it had been as easy as that. Roberts had been better than his word. He had made the recommendation before Henry had asked for it, and after only a few short days of unemployment, Henry Starr found himself back at work cowboying again, still not too far from the rented cabin of the Morrisons. The world seemed all right to Henry. He had a job doing the kind of work that he enjoyed, being around the kind of people he could understand, and he had a sweetheart—the prettiest gal he could ever remember seeing anywhere. Life was just fine.

3

The new job was just fine, too. Henry liked Charles Todd, and he got along well with all the cowboys on the Todd Ranch, even though they were all, like those on the Roberts Ranch, white. He began to think that perhaps he would be forced to revise his opinion of white men. Perhaps, after all, C. N. Walker and Clint Chambers were not the typical ones. Anyhow, Henry liked the life and work of a cowboy, and he was happy with the job at Todd's. Mae was pleased, too, for she hadn't liked seeing Henry footloose. She was glad to see him back at work and still close to her. Besides all that, it was branding time, and Henry particularly liked branding.

He was at work with a small branding crew, holding onto the hind legs of a hefty young calf while two other cowboys held down the front end. A fourth brought the red-hot branding iron out of the fire and pressed it against the side of the calf. Henry listened to the calf bawl and smelled the burning hair. Then his two partners turned loose of the head and front legs, and Henry let go of his hold. The calf struggled frantically to its feet and ran bawling for its mother. As Henry was about to turn to his next chore, Charles Todd rode into the branding camp.

"Howdy, Mr. Todd," said Henry.

"Henry," said Todd, "ride over to that east pasture. There's a couple of stray horses in there. Someone will probably be looking for them pretty soon, so let them through the gate to water. We can hold them there until we find out who belongs to them."

Henry found the strays with no problem and let them through the gate as Todd had instructed him to do. He noted that they were fine-looking animals. Todd had been right, he figured. They were bound to be missed by their owner. At least he would find them well cared for. That was just one of the things that Henry liked about the ranch life. People looked out for each other—even in a case like this where they didn't know whose horses they had found. It didn't matter, really, he figured. It was like the Golden Rule. You did for the other fellow what you hoped that he would do for you if you wound up in the same kind of fix.

It was a couple of weeks later when Henry, lying on his bunk in the big bunkhouse that housed all the cowboys, and playing on his fiddle some old tune he didn't even know the title of, was visited by Charles Todd. Todd had brought another man along with him. It was unusual enough for the boss to come into the bunkhouse in the late evening, but it was a rare occasion indeed for him to bring a stranger. Henry stopped sawing on the fiddle, and all the cowboys quieted down so as to overhear what they could. It wasn't exactly eavesdropping. They were just curious about so rare an occurrence, and, after all, the bunkhouse was their home.

Todd had led the stranger directly over to Henry. Henry put aside the fiddle and stood up.

"Henry," said Todd.

"Yes, sir, Mr. Todd?"

"Henry, this here is Hank Eaton. He asked me to bring him in here to meet you."

Henry extended his right hand, wondering who this stranger might be and what possible interest he could have in Henry. The other man took it warmly in his own.

"Mr. Eaton owns them two horses you penned up a while back," said Todd.

"Oh," said Henry. "Well, how do you do, Mr. Eaton?"

"I just wanted to thank you, young man, for watching out for them two horses the way you done," said Eaton. "I been missing them for near a month, and I sure am pleased to find them in such good shape. I'd like to pay you something for your trouble."

Eaton reached into a pocket, but Henry stopped him before he could dig out any cash.

"You don't owe me anything, Mr. Eaton," he said. "I was drawing wages from Mr. Todd, here, when I put them in. I'm not out anything. Just glad to help."

Eaton thanked Henry again and left with Charles Todd. Henry picked up the fiddle and watched while the two other men left the bunkhouse. He lay back down on the bunk with a good, warm feeling inside.

But it was only a few days later when Todd sent Henry with a wagon into Nowata to pick up some supplies. Henry had parked the wagon in front of the grain store and gone inside to pick up the supplies Todd had ordered. It was going to take several trips out to the wagon to load everything up. He hefted a grain sack up onto his shoulder and hauled it outside. As he rolled his shoulder to pitch the sack into the wagon bed, a man he had never seen before approached him.

"Henry Starr?" he said.

Henry looked up at the man. He was a bit short, perhaps five feet six or seven, and paunchy. A shaggy moustache covered his mouth. He wore what would have passed for dress clothes had they been cleaned and pressed, but they were wrinkled and covered with dust. His dusty hat looked as if it had been thrown in the street and rolled on. His trousers were stuffed into the tops of his high black boots. There were two cartridge belts around the man's wide waist, and into the belts were stuffed two big revolvers. A badge was pinned carelessly to the coat.

"Yeah?" said Henry.

The man pulled a paper out of a coat pocket and casually waved it in front of Henry's eyes.

"I have here a writ," he said, "charging you with the larceny of a horse belonging to a Mr. Hank Eaton. I'm a deputy United States marshal, and you're under arrest."

Henry was too startled to give an immediate reply. He looked at the deputy with unbelieving eyes for a second or two. He knew he had broken no laws and wondered how such a mistake could have been made.

"Wait a minute," he finally managed to say. "There must be some mistake. I took care of two strays for Mr. Eaton, but other than that, I've never laid eyes on his horse. He'll straighten this out. Him or Mr. Todd one. I work for Mr. Todd, and he was there when Eaton thanked me for taking care of his horses. He even offered to pay me. You ask him."

"This here writ is signed by Hank Eaton," said the deputy. "Come along."

The ruddy-faced, paunchy man grabbed Henry by a wrist, and before Henry could take in what was happening, he was wearing a pair of handcuffs and being pushed along the road toward a nearby hotel. He could feel the stares of the curious onlookers as he moved along the street, and he wanted to turn and yell at them all that he hadn't done anything wrong. This deputy was making a bad mistake.

About halfway to the hotel from where he had left the Todd wagon, he spoke to the deputy again.

"Let me send word out to the ranch where I work," he said, "so they'll know where I'm at."

The dusty man gave him a rude shove toward the hotel.

"You move along, boy," he said.

Henry knew that something was terribly wrong, but he couldn't think of anything he could do about it. He walked ahead of the deputy, who gave him an occasional push to maintain his pace and direction. Soon the deputy had shoved him through the front door of the hotel and, ignoring the desk and the sleepy man behind it, on up the stairs. There in the hallway before a door to one of the rooms, Hank Eaton stood, looking nervous and sheepish.

"Mr. Eaton," said Henry, "what . . . ?"

Eaton turned his head to avoid Henry's look, but he needn't have bothered. The deputy didn't allow Henry to finish his question, and Henry had gotten a good enough look at Eaton to see on his long, thin face not only embarrassment, but also shame and guilt. The man obviously knew what he was doing. Henry wished that he knew. The deputy shoved Henry through the doorway into the room.

"Get inside, boy," he said.

Staying out in the hall with Eaton, the deputy closed the door and locked it, leaving Henry alone and handcuffed inside the shabby hotel room. Henry stood just inside the door, feeling thoroughly bewildered and helpless, and through the door he heard the voice of the deputy.

"You stand guard here until I get back."

Alone and pacing the floor, Henry had plenty of time to get over his initial bewilderment and become indignant. He knew that he had done nothing wrong. In fact, Henry Starr took pride in his strong sense of honor and of right. Though the Starrs were a mixed-blood family, the Cherokee concept of *duyukduh* was firmly ingrained in their sense of values: *duyukduh*—a word that the English "right" or "justice" does not begin to translate adequately. In Henry's mind, a man who had been arrested had brought shame and humiliation not only on himself but on his family. And here he was locked in a hotel room by a deputy United States marshal and wearing handcuffs like a common criminal. He was angry and embarrassed at the same time. His original notion concerning the general worth of the white race was coming back stronger than ever.

Henry was left a good long while to stew. It was beginning to get dark before he heard a key turn in the lock on the door. He was sitting on the edge of the bed, and he decided not to jump up and appear anxious as the deputy entered the room. He sat and glared at the man, waiting for him to make any next move. He felt almost certain that the deputy was about to make an abject apology to him and try to explain how he had made such a terrible error. He was disappointed, for the paunchy lawman said nothing to him at all. Instead, he simply walked indifferently across the room to Henry and shoved a tin plate under his nose. Henry took the plate. It had on it a hunk of sausage and a few crackers. Henry thought briefly of shoving the plate back or of tossing it to the floor, but he was hungry. The sausage was cold and greasy and the crackers were stale, but he ate them. The deputy watched without saying a word, until Henry was finished, then he walked back over to the bed, took the empty plate away from Henry, tossed it aside, and reached into his vest pocket for a key. He unlocked the cuffs from one of Henry's wrists, and locked the other wrist to the iron bedstead. Then he went back out into the hallway, locking the door behind him once again.

Henry wondered if the man was somehow worried that he might drag the whole bed through the doorway and thus escape. Through the door, he could hear low voices, the deputy's and Eaton's, he supposed, but he could not make out anything that they were saying. After a while, in spite of the circumstances, he drifted off to a fitful sleep, filled with images of criminals, lawmen, cheap hotel rooms, and dank jail cells. But worst of all, he found himself walking down the main street of town, the sidewalks on either side of him lined with people he knew, his mother and C.N., the Morrisons and Mae, Mr. Roberts, Mr. Todd, and as he walked past them, each one turned his head away in shame.

4

Henry slept fitfully, and he was awake the following morning early when the deputy arrived. He heard him in the hallway, kicking and talking loudly to someone, presumably Eaton.

"Wake up," Henry heard him say. "We got a long ride ahead of us."

Then Henry heard the key turn in the lock again, and soon the door opened and the deputy made his appearance. He wore the same wretched clothes he had worn the day before. Henry figured the man had slept in them. He wondered how long it had been since this white man had taken a bath. He seemed as unconcerned as ever as he brought out his key to the manacles and approached Henry.

"Where are you taking me?" demanded Henry.

The deputy unlocked the wrist that was fastened to the bedstead and hooked Henry's two wrists back together.

"The court at Fort Smith," he said nonchalantly.

Henry had heard of the court at Fort Smith and the famous hanging judge, Isaac Parker. He didn't think that Judge Parker would hang him, but the knowledge of where he was being taken did put fear into his heart, and he had learned that he would get nowhere with this great clod of a man by demanding justice or by protesting his innocence, so he followed along quietly.

Soon the three of them—Henry, the deputy, and the sleazy Eaton—were riding horseback across the prairies of the northern Cherokee Nation. Henry maintained his silence for a good, long while. He was riding on his own horse and in his own saddle, and he wondered how the deputy had obtained them, as Henry had driven into Nowata in the wagon, leaving his horse and saddle back at the Todd Ranch. Finally he could no longer contain himself.

"I'm telling you," he shouted as they rode along the trail, "I haven't done anything. Mr. Eaton, what's this all about?"

Eaton kept his eyes straight forward. He didn't answer. Henry thought that it appeared as if Eaton didn't have the guts to look him in the eyes. At least that was some indication that the man had a semblance of a conscience, but Henry couldn't figure out a motive for what Eaton was doing to him. Eaton didn't answer, but the deputy did.

"Listen, boy," he said, "I don't know what you've done or what you ain't done. All I do is serve the writs. The court decides whether you're guilty or not."

"How did you get my horse?" said Henry.

"That's all right," said the deputy. "I got him, didn't I?"

Once again Henry resolved to remain silent, and he maintained that silence the rest of what seemed to him to be the longest day of his life. Eventually the deputy called a halt to the ride and made a sloppy camp beside a stream for the night. He heated up some beans over a fire that Henry thought was large enough to roast a good-sized hog over, and he gave Henry a small dab of them. He also boiled some coffee and served it around. Eaton had still refused to speak to Henry and continued to avoid his gaze. After finishing his coffee, the deputy suddenly decided to move around the fire and sit down beside Henry. He spoke with what sounded to Henry like feigned concern.

"You ever been to Fort Smith before?" he said.

"No."

"You ever been arrested?"

"No."

Henry's second negative reply was louder than the first and filled with obvious and intentional indignation. The deputy sniffed loudly and spat toward the fire. He leaned back on an elbow.

"Look, boy," he said, "like I told you before, I don't know if you stole that man's horse or not. I'm just doing my job. But I can see that you're scared, and you got a reason to be. Young fella like you—never been in trouble before. Don't know your way around with courts and judges and all that. Hell, you could be innocent and still wind up in jail and never know what happened to you."

The deputy paused to let his words soak in. He settled back even more and groaned as he did. He glanced at Henry to see if he could detect the impact of his words on the young man's face. Seeing nothing there, he continued.

"Tell you what," he said. "I'll do this much for you. When we get to Fort Smith, I'll stop off with you at a lawyer's office—that is, if you want me to. You're going to need someone on your side. Especially you being Indian and all. I tell you what. I sure wouldn't want to be going up in front of Judge Parker. No sir. Not me. Not Isaac C. Parker."

The deputy's speech had made its impact on the young cowboy, though Henry had been careful not to let it show. He found himself, for the second night in a row, tired, bewildered, afraid, and unable to sleep. He supposed that he would have to let the deputy introduce him to a lawyer. What other recourse had he? He knew no one in Fort Smith, and, so far as he knew, there was no one in the world besides his two unwanted companions who knew where he was. He wondered, even if he could manage to extricate himself from this outlandish mess, whether or not he would have a job when he got back to the Todd Ranch. Guilty or innocent, he thought, it really didn't matter much once a man had been arrested. Being in jail is no excuse for missing work.

Once they arrived in Fort Smith, the deputy, true to his word, took Henry directly to the office of an attorney-at-law. They tied their horses to a hitching rail in front of the building, and the deputy led Henry, still manacled, into the office. It was small, cluttered, and dusty. A fat, perspiring redheaded man sat puffing a cigar behind a desk. He looked up when Henry and the deputy came into his office, and, ignoring Henry, he smiled and stood up to greet the deputy.

"Oh, hello, Bernie," he said.

"Howdy, John."

"You look like you've had a hard ride," said the lawyer, puffing smoke.

"Not too bad," said the deputy. "I may have a customer for you here."

"We call them clients, Bernie," said the lawyer. "What did he do?"

"I didn't do anything," said Henry.

The lawyer didn't seem even to acknowledge Henry's protestation, though he did rephrase his question.

"What is he alleged to have done?"

"He's supposed to have stole a horse," said the deputy.

"Any evidence?"

"The man that owns the horse signed a writ against him. I got it right here."

The deputy showed the document to the lawyer, who studied it hastily, puffing all the while.

"Well, boy," he said, "it appears to me that you sure do need some legal representation. You got any money?"

Henry reached into his pocket with some difficulty because of the handcuffs and pulled out all his cash, which he dumped onto the lawyer's desk. The fat man counted it quickly and greedily.

"Twenty-two dollars," he said. "Is that all you got?"

"Every last penny," said Henry.

The lawyer scraped it off the desk into a fat palm and pocketed it. He looked up at the deputy.

"Whose horse is he riding?" he asked.

"That's my horse," said Henry. He was beginning to be sick of these two talking about him as if he were not even in the room.

"It's his," said the deputy.

"Well," puffed the lawyer, looking out his office window toward the hitching rail, "he'll fetch a few dollars. What about the saddle?"

"It's mine," said Henry. "It's nearly brand-new. I paid forty dollars for it."

The big redhead moved back around behind his desk and dropped with a heavy sigh into his well-worn office chair. He leaned back with a creak and puffed out great clouds of smoke.

"These things cost money," he said. "I can't get very far for you with twenty-two dollars, but, uh, if you'll sign this bill of sale for your horse and saddle, I might be able to help you out."

"Even if you do get me out of this, how am I going to get home from here without my horse?"

"You're a long ways from out," said the redhead. "First things first."

"Where else you going to turn, boy?" said the deputy.

Henry felt sick. He didn't like either of these two men, and he didn't trust them. He felt certain that they were just trying to get his money, and he felt like a fool for handing it over. Now they wanted his horse and saddle. He felt terribly young and inexperienced all of a sudden, and he felt completely vulnerable. This was all wrong, but he had no place else to turn. He had no idea what to do. He was alone and lost and almost without hope. Henry signed the paper.

5

The jail guard shoved Henry Starr roughly into the large cell in the Fort Smith jail and shut the heavy door behind him with a clank. Henry could hear the large key turn in the lock as he looked around himself to take in his new setting. The cell was large, yet it was overcrowded. The prisoners all seemed to be looking at him, and they were a rough and seedy-looking lot. Henry thought that he had never before in his life seen so many of the lowest type of humanity in one crowded location. They were filthy, as was the cell into which they were packed, and Henry was nearly overcome by the oppressive stench that pervaded the atmosphere of the place. In spite of the chaos into which he had just been so rudely thrust, Henry noticed that one prisoner did not seem to be paying attention to his entrance. That man was lounging on a filthy cot against the far wall. He appeared to be a large man, and he was obviously a full-blooded Indian.

Henry had just barely taken in all this when one of the prisoners jumped up from where he crouched against the moldy wall and shouted.

"Fresh fish. Fresh fish."

Suddenly the cell was all movement. The prisoners were all running around, and a number of them laid hands on Henry and dragged him across the room. When they had him where they wanted him and the dragging and shoving had more or less stopped, Henry saw that he had been placed before a particularly scroungy-looking convict who was perched on an upper-level bunk and leering down at him. A small, weasel-faced man at the foot of the bunk stood up in mock formality and squealed out as loudly as he could.

"Oh, yes. Oh, yes. The honorable kangaroo court is now in session."

The prisoners became disturbingly quiet. Henry had no idea what was about to befall him. He braced himself for the worst. Then the wretch on the top bunk spoke in a solemn voice.

"Sheriff," he intoned, "what is this prisoner charged with?"

"Why, judge, your honor," answered another, "breaking into our jail without permission."

The decorum of the court broke down as the prisoners all began to shout, "Guilty. Guilty." The judge allowed this to go on for a bit before deciding to regain control.

"Order," he finally shouted above the din. "Order, or I'll have to clear this courtroom."

The mob of prisoners roared with laughter. This time the judge prudently waited until the laughter died down before continuing.

"I find this prisoner guilty of breaking into jail," he said, "and fine him fifty cents for the offense."

"Pay up, prisoner," ordered the sheriff.

"I haven't got fifty cents," said Henry.

The judge looked hurt.

"What do you got?" he said.

Henry pulled his trouser pockets inside out.

"I haven't got a cent," he said. "A real criminal, better known as a lawyer, got to me before you did."

A few of the prisoners giggled at Henry's characterization of the lawyer, but the judge was still looking pained. Then the sheriff noticed Henry's right hand, grabbed the wrist and pulled it up for the judge's view.

"He's got a gold ring," he shouted.

The judge's pained expression left his face at once. His watery eyes lit up just a bit beneath their reddish tint.

"Gold? Ah, the court will hold it for security," he decreed.

The sheriff reached for the ring to try to pull it off Henry's finger, but Henry shot out a quick left hook that crushed some cartilage in the sheriff's nose. The sheriff howled, grabbed for his face, and sank down on his knees. Henry didn't wait for the others to react. As soon as the sheriff released his right wrist, Henry swung a right at the nearest chin. Knowing that he was not only outnumbered, but also, in effect, surrounded, he spun around so that his back was to the judge, reached up over his shoulders, and, taking the judge totally by surprise, threw him out into the crowd of scrambling prisoners. At least, with that move, he would have no one at his back. The mob moved in on him, and Henry took a couple of glancing blows to the side of his head, but there were just too many hands reaching for him. He knew that he couldn't last long against them.

Then a scream came from in back of the crowd, and a prisoner went flying through the room to crash against a wall. The big, quiet Indian had gotten up and joined the fray. Before the crowd realized what was happening, he had knocked two more of their number out of the fight. The odds were much improved, and Henry fought back with renewed determination. He was actually, to his own astonishment, enjoying it. After so much frustration, after such a long time of feeling utterly helpless, he found himself with a means of releasing his tensions. He had someone to strike back at.

Then a guard stepped in at the door and fired a pistol shot into the ceiling, and the fight was over.

Henry felt a little better after the fight, but even that didn't help when he looked around for a place to sit down and try to relax. The big Indian had gone back to his spot on the filthy cot and showed no inclination to talk to Henry. It was as if the fight had never taken place. Henry had never seen such filth in his life as what he found in this Fort Smith jail, and he felt suddenly unclean just being in the cell. It was bad enough to have the soles of his boots on the putrid floor, and he certainly didn't want to touch anything with any other part of his body or clothing.

As the day dragged on into the night, though, he found that his weariness overcame him, and he had to lie down. Only after he settled did he notice the bugs. He was awake long after all the others had gone to sleep, and, thinking about what had befallen him, breathing the foul, stale air of the cell, he finally fell asleep with tears running down his cheeks.

6

Henry spent the next two weeks in the cell at Fort Smith. His lawyer did not come to see him. He didn't see the deputy again. He saw no one except the prisoners and the guards who brought the food to the cell. The other prisoners left him alone after the fight, and, even though he had come to Henry's defense, the big Indian still kept to himself. Henry had lost track of time, and he had begun to feel as if he would never see the light of day again. He had gotten to the point where he didn't even bother to look at the floor or a cot or the wall before sitting, lying down, or leaning back. He had been so long in the filth that he had become adjusted to it. He no longer noticed the fetid atmosphere of the cell.

He was, like the others, a little curious when the cell door was opened one morning and it was too early yet for the noon meal. The guard who opened the door didn't go into the cell. He just opened the door a little, stuck his head in, and yelled out.

"Henry Starr?"

Henry stood up slowly, cautiously, his head filled with fear and apprehension and suspicion of everyone he had encountered in Fort Smith. Inside he wanted to jump and run. He didn't know what to expect, but anything would be better than the sitting and waiting in filth—filth that he had almost ceased to notice. He might be going to trial, for all he knew, or it might be the slimy lawyer finally come to consult with him. He had no idea what might be in store for him as he walked toward the doorway. All he knew was that he wanted out of the cell, out of the filth, away from the hardened, unfeeling criminals, the living corpses, the less than human monsters who inhabited this unearthly environment.

"Come on out," said the guard.

Henry stepped out into the hallway. Even there, still inside the jail, the air felt cleaner. There beside the guard was Charlie Starr, Henry's Uncle Charlie, brother of old Hop Starr. Henry was suddenly painfully aware of his own filth. He wondered how much he, himself, stank to someone who had been outside living in the real world. He was in one sense overjoyed at the sight of his uncle, but at the same time he was humiliated and ashamed. He wanted out of the jail, but he also wanted to hide from his uncle. He had a shocking realization that a part of him, something inside, wanted to hide so badly that it actually created an impulse to run back into the hated cell.

"Uncle Charlie," said Henry, his voice betraying his astonishment. "Uncle Charlie, how did you—?"

Charlie Starr cut him off short.

"Come on, Henry," he said. "Let's get out of here. We'll talk later."

Whatever had to be done to get Henry released from jail had apparently already been taken care of by his uncle, for Charlie Starr led Henry directly outside and to a hitching rail where he had two saddled horses waiting. He untied one and handed the reins to Henry without a word. Henry mounted up, and Charlie climbed on the other horse and led the way out of town.

He rode in silence for a good way out into the countryside, then led Henry off the road down a trail to a campsite beside a creek. Undoing his saddle roll, he produced a bar of lye soap and a new suit of clothes. Henry took the soap, stripped, and rushed into the clear, cold water. He was glad for the strong lye soap, and he almost used up the entire bar scrubbing himself over and over until his skin was nearly raw. He washed his hair again and again until he felt reasonably certain there were no bugs settled in there. The water felt good. It felt clean. And the air was fresh.

Henry felt as if he could stay in that fresh water much longer, but his curiosity was tormenting him ferociously. He got out and dried off, put on his fresh clothes, and felt almost normal again. He was still ashamed. He had done nothing to deserve it, but he had been in jail. The humiliation, unlike the filth and the stench, would not wash off.

While Henry had been scraping his skin in the creek, Charlie Starr had built a small fire and pulled out of his saddle pack some bean bread and some coffee. He boiled the coffee grounds in a small pot he had set on the fire and, when Henry finally came out of the creek, passed him the bread. After two weeks of Fort Smith jail slop, Henry was glad to taste anything from outside. He relished the traditional Cherokee bread, and the pure, cold creek water, with which he washed it down, was delicious. He politely refused the coffee. When he had satisfied his palate and his stomach, he decided that it was time to try to satisfy his curiosity.

"Uncle Charlie," he said, "how did you know where to find me?"

"I guess one of Todd's cowboys was in town and seen you arrested. Anyhow, Todd sent the man to tell me."

"Then Mr. Todd knows where I've been," said Henry, staring into the fire and watching the small licks of flame dance.

"He knows, Henry, and he knows that you're innocent. I went by to see him on my way here after you. He told me about that damned coward, Eaton, and his horses. Don't worry. You've still got a job."

"What about the trial and all that?" asked Henry.

"There won't be any trial," said Charlie, reaching for the coffeepot and refilling his cup. "I found Eaton still in

Fort Smith and made it clear to him that I wouldn't put up with him swearing a lie on you in court, so he finally told them that there was after all a doubt in his mind whether you had actually stole his horse. It took a little doing, but I finally got it straightened out. I've learned how to play this white man's game pretty well by now."

That was an understatement. Charlie Starr was a wealthy man. The Starr Ranch made both Roberts' and Todd's look like jerkwater outfits. And Charlie dressed the part of a rich rancher, too.

Henry took a cold sip of creek water.

"I spent two weeks in that stink hole," he said, "and I'm innocent. Where's the justice in that? Eaton should be charged with perjury or something."

"Let it go, Henry," advised his uncle. "You're free."

Henry got to his feet and paced around to the other side of the fire.

"But, Uncle Charlie," he said, "they treated me like a common criminal. Like a murderer. Why? Why did Eaton do that to me after I looked after his horses?"

"Sit down and try to relax," snapped the old rancher. "Henry, when that deputy put you in jail, he got one hundred and twenty-five dollars. Then he got forty dollars for mileage. He got fifty cents a meal for feeding you three meals a day while on the way here."

"He gave me one hunk of sausage and some crackers, was all. One meal—if you could call it that."

He didn't bother to mention the spoonful of beans.

"Eaton got twenty dollars for mileage and a buck fifty a day while waiting in Fort Smith for your trial," continued Charlie, "and they probably got a cut of what that lawyer took from you."

"You mean they just used me to make some extra money? They arrest people for that? Just to make money, and they don't care whether a man's guilty or not?"

"Pocket money, I believe they call it," said Charlie. "You were handy."

"Well, Uncle Charlie, it's not right. Remember back a few years—how different things were? Back then we looked down on white people. Now it's the other way around."

Charlie Starr sighed. Of course, he could remember back a good many more years than could his nephew, but he had, he believed, learned to accept things the way they were. That didn't mean that he had to like them. It just meant that he knew when to fight back and when not to. Some things, Charlie knew, couldn't be changed. But he could also remember the impetuousness of youth and the idealism, and he felt sorry for his nephew having to learn a lesson about the world in such a hard way.

"Yeah," he said, "things have really changed from the days when the only whites in the Cherokee Nation were wagonloads of poor white trash moving in one week and out the next. It's a different breed now."

"A different breed, huh?" said Henry. "Well, they're still trash."

Charlie spread his blanket and tossed one to Henry. Then he sat down to pull off his boots.

"Just try to put it out of your mind, Henry," he said. "When we get back home, go back to work and just forget all this."

Charlie rolled over on his side and settled himself into the ground to sleep. It was obvious to Henry that his uncle had said his last word on the subject. Henry picked up the blanket he had been tossed, but he didn't immediately spread it on the ground. He stood looking at the form of his uncle there before him, and when he spoke, it was more to himself than to Charlie.

"Forget it?" he said.

Henry turned his back on his uncle and paced a few steps away. He was feeling exasperated with the old man.

He was grateful to Charlie for his rescue, but Charlie was shrugging it all off much too easily for Henry's sense of terrible injustice. He spread the blanket on the ground and sat down on it, his elbows on his knees, his chin in the palms of his hands. There was a rage inside Henry Starr, and he couldn't figure out what to do with it. Finally he stretched out on the blanket, and in spite of his internal wrath and turmoil, he was soon asleep in the fresh night air. It was the first restful sleep he had experienced since his arrest in Nowata.

7

Henry did go back to work at the Todd Ranch, but it just wasn't the same. No one ever said anything or did anything related to Henry's scrape with the law, but Henry felt as if they all looked at him just a bit differently. He couldn't quite nail it down. It was just a feeling that he had. Maybe, he thought, it was just his imagination, but he didn't really believe that. He did his work, and he spent his off time mostly in the bunkhouse with his fiddle. His fiddle tunes were always the mournful ones.

One evening as he moped in the bunkhouse, Charles Todd came in to see him.

"Henry," he said, "there's someone up at the house to see you."

Henry carefully laid aside his fiddle and bow and got up off his bunk.

"Who is it?" he asked.

"Why don't you just run on over there and find out?"

On the large front porch of the ranch house, Henry found Mae Morrison waiting for him. His feelings were mixed, for he had missed her desperately, yet he was ashamed. For an instant he thought of running away to hide from her, but before he could do that, Mae had seen him. He had to face her. He walked on up and stood close to the porch.

"Hello, Henry," she said. "Remember me?"

"Hello, Mae," said Henry, digging the toe of his boot into the ground and avoiding her eyes. "I . . . ."

"Why didn't you come to see me?"

"I wanted to, Mae. I really did. But I was—I don't know—too ashamed, I guess. I've been in jail, Mae, for stealing a horse. With criminals. Real criminals. I'm a convict."

Mae walked over to Henry and slowly put her arms around his shoulders. Henry still avoided her eyes, and she shook him gently.

"Henry," she said, "no one who knows you believes that. And they let you go, didn't they? It was all just a bad mistake. Don't let it bother you anymore. Okay?"

For a moment Henry's voice caught in his throat, and his eyes felt watery. He was glad that tears didn't run down his cheeks. He took a couple of deep breaths to maintain his composure. Then he allowed Mae's gentle pull to draw him up close to her in an embrace. He put his arms around her and held her tight.

"Okay," he said.

"Don't keep hiding from me."

"I won't anymore."

Mae stepped back from Henry, a little embarrassed because of the setting. She smiled.

"Henry," she said, "I've got to be getting back home before it gets too late."

"How'd you get here?" he asked.

"Papa let me ride old Jeff," she said, nodding toward the fence at the far end of the porch.

Henry glanced after her nod and saw Jeff Davis, Mr. Morrison's old workhorse, nonchalantly grazing at the clumps of grass at his feet. He wore no saddle.

"I'll borrow a saddle horse and a saddle for you," he said, "and I'll ride back with you. Just sit down here and relax for a few minutes, and I'll be right back. Okay?"

Charlie Todd let Henry borrow a horse and saddle for Mae, and Henry saddled up that one and his own, the one his uncle had brought to him to ride back from Fort Smith. As Henry had been swindled out of his own horse and saddle by the redheaded lawyer in Fort Smith, his uncle had made him a gift of the other. Soon Mae and Henry were riding toward the Morrison home, leading Jeff Davis. For Henry the ride was all too short, but it was late and Mae had to get inside. They put Jeff Davis away, and Henry walked Mae up to the house.

"Thank you for coming to see me," he said. "I do feel a lot better."

"Will you come over and see me on Sunday, Henry?"

"Nothing could keep me away now, Mae," said Henry. "I'll be here."

As he rode back toward the Todd Ranch, Henry sat light in the saddle. Things seemed to be working out all right. He had, indeed, had a bad time, and it had been all undeserved. Yet his friends and his relatives, his employer, all knew that he had not been to blame. Perhaps, after all, he should feel good that he was known and liked well enough to have withstood the stigma of the Fort Smith jail and the charge of horse stealing. Not just anyone would have been able to overcome those things as well as he had, he thought. It was amazing how much better the closeness of Mae had made him feel. He could see now that he need not have stayed away from her all that time. He should have known how she would react.

Henry still felt good the following morning when the boss sent him into town in the wagon to pick up some new rolls of wire. Todd had noticed that Henry had been confining himself pretty much to the ranch until Mae had come around, and he had decided that it would be good for the young man to make the trip into town. The last time Henry had gone to town, he had gotten into trouble. The way Todd looked at it, it was the same thing as getting back on a horse after a man has been thrown. He also wanted Henry to know that he still trusted him, that he hadn't put any stock in that charge of Eaton's. So he had purposely picked Henry out to send on the errand to town, and he had been pleased to find Henry willing, even eager, to make the trip. It looked to Todd, too, as if things were going to be all right.

Henry was about halfway to town when he heard a rider coming up behind him on the road, and he heard his name called. He pulled the wagon to a halt and turned in the seat to see who was coming. He recognized the rider as Tump Collins, a man he knew from hanging around Nowata. They were not good friends, just mere acquaintances. Henry sat and waited for Collins to ride up beside the wagon. Collins seemed to be in a hurry, and he was carrying in his left hand a valise.

"Hello, Tump," said Henry. "You seem to be in a big hurry to get somewhere."

"Yeah," said Collins. "I'm supposed to meet someone about a job. Say, are you headed into town?"

"Yeah. Running an errand for the boss."

"Well, listen, Henry, you'd do me a real favor if you'd let me toss this here grip in your wagon and haul it into town for me. It sure is awkward toting it around like this."

"What do I do with it when I get to town?"

"Just leave it for me at the hotel. They know me. I'll pick it up there later. Okay?"

"Sure," said Henry.

Collins reached over and set the valise down in the wagon bed, then he touched the brim of his hat and nodded to Henry as he began to turn his horse.

"Thanks," he said, and he rode off back in the direction he had come from.

Henry flicked the reins and resumed his drive to town. He had gone only another mile or so when he once again heard the sound of hooves behind him. He glanced over his shoulder again and this time saw two riders coming hard. He turned his attention back to the road so as to keep the wagon to one side and allow the riders to pass easily. After a moment he glanced again back to see how close they were getting, and this time he could see them more clearly. They were both white men. Henry did not recognize them, but he could see that they were holding revolvers in their hands. When the riders came up alongside the wagon, they slowed their mounts and pointed the pistols at Henry. He stopped the wagon again and set the hand brake.

"Hold it, there. Pull up," shouted one of the riders.

"What's this all about?" said Henry.

"We're deputy United States marshals," said the second rider.

Henry felt a moment of panic surge through his body as the speaker climbed down off his horse and stepped over to the wagon. The man tucked his pistol into his waistband and reached over the wagon box to pick up the valise that Collins had deposited there. He opened it up to reveal its contents to his partner, who was still holding his gun on Henry.

"Whiskey," said the still-mounted deputy.

"Whiskey?" said Henry. "Hey, I didn't have any idea what was in that grip."

"Say, Homer," said the man holding the valise, "he says he didn't even know what's in here."

"Naw," said Homer in mock disbelief.

"I don't even drink whiskey," said Henry.

"In that case," said Homer, "you must have intended to sell it, and that makes the charge against you more serious. Slap the cuffs on him, Pete."

Pete replaced the valise in the wagon and reached under his dusty coat for a pair of handcuffs.

"Not again," said Henry, a little more loudly than he had intended.

"Oh," said Pete, "you been arrested before?"

"Yeah, but I was innocent."

"That's what they all say," said Pete. "Stick your hands out here."

Henry obeyed.

"Where are you taking me? To Fort Smith?"

"Nope," said Homer. "Whiskey court in Muskogee."

With Henry's wrists cuffed, he couldn't be expected to drive the wagon, so Pete climbed up on the seat beside him to drive.

"Bring my horse, Homer?" he said.

"Sure."

Pete whipped up the team and the wagon moved along down the road. Homer took the reins of Pete's horse in his hand and climbed into his own saddle, but then he just sat there as if he were waiting for someone else. Pretty soon another rider appeared from around the bend to his rear and loped his horse up casually to stop beside Homer. It was the deputy called Bernie, the one who had first arrested Henry on false charges in Nowata. He smiled and touched the brim of his battered hat.

"I'm obliged, Homer," he said.

"That's all right," said Homer. "Hell, we can't be letting these damned Indians think they can get the best of the law."

8

Henry took his second brush with the law a bit more in stride. To begin with, Muskogee was not as far away from home as was Fort Smith. In fact, Muskogee was less than a dozen miles from the home of Henry's mother near Fort Gibson. In the second place, Henry knew from his first experience that Uncle Charlie Starr not only could, but would, help him out of a jam, and from the jail in Muskogee, Henry found it relatively simple to get word to his uncle. The jail, though far from pleasant, was much more easily endured than was the one at Fort Smith, and, finally, though it was certainly frustrating for Henry to have been accused wrongly a second time, his first experience taught him that he could get out of the troublesome situation and recover from it. In short, although he was angry at the mistreatment he was receiving at the hands of the federal authorities, he was also just a bit cocky. He was a veteran.

Uncle Charlie did show up, and he did get Henry out of the cell. This time, however, Henry would have to go to court, and this time Charlie Starr had a different kind of advice.

"I advise you to plead guilty, Henry," he said, "and pay the fine."

"But, Uncle Charlie, I didn't do anything."

"This time, Henry, you got no case. You was arrested by two deputies—not one—two. You was alone, and they found whiskey on you."

"It wasn't on me, Uncle Charlie. It was in the wagon,

and I told you how it got there. I didn't even know what it was."

"Henry," said Charlie, "it's your word against theirs. Two lawmen. There wasn't nobody else around. You are, in fact, guilty of having that stuff in your possession. There is no way we can even argue against that."

"It was a setup," said Henry. "Someone's out to get me because of Uncle Sam and Grandpa."

Charlie Starr rubbed his fists into his eyes and turned away from his nephew. He knew that there was a possibility that Henry might be right. He didn't really think that was what was happening, but it had happened before. Old Tom Starr, father of Charlie and Sam and Hop, was said to have killed a hundred men. His father, James, had been one of the signers of the Treaty of New Echota, the fraudulent treaty by which the United States Government justified the removal of the entire Cherokee Nation from their ancestral homelands in what had become North and South Carolina, Georgia, Alabama, Tennessee, and other Southern states. The treaty signers had been blamed by other tribal members for the misery of the Trail of Tears, and after the bitter trail, treaty signers, including Major Ridge, John Ridge, Elias Boudinot, and James Starr, had been brutally assassinated. Tom had witnessed the killing of his father and had vowed revenge, and the bloody trail he left behind him insured the entire Starr family more than its share of enemies.

Tom Starr had lived to a ripe old age, and even before his death, his son Sam had added to the notoriety of the family by his marriage to a white woman named Myra Belle Shirley. She had become famous as Belle Starr, and Belle and Sam, Henry's Uncle Sam, were rumored to be involved in a large-scale horse stealing operation. There were dime novels out circulating all over the country about the Starrs, particularly about Belle, but Sam and even Old Tom were frequently mentioned in the tales. It

was a family reputation that was not always easy to live
with. Henry particularly resented the fact that his family
name was beginning to be associated widely with a white
woman. Some of the dime novels he had seen did not even
make mention of the fact that Belle's husband, Sam, was
Indian. He appeared as a white man.

At any rate, Charlie Starr knew that there were people
who would do almost anything to get to the Starrs. He
knew that Henry had nothing to do with the revenge pattern of Old Tom or with the activities of Sam and Belle,
but he also knew that to some, none of that would make
any difference. In fact, according to Charlie's experience
with the world, there were a good many people who
would seek revenge or assuage their jealousies by purpose-
fully seeking out the seeming most vulnerable and de-
fenseless member of a family.

Charlie turned back on Henry with a surprising fierce-
ness in his look.

"I don't think so, Henry," he said. "Most of that's long
over. More likely, one of two things happened. Either that
fellow who dumped the whiskey on you knew that there
were some deputies around and he needed to get rid of it
quick and found you handy, or maybe he was in cahoots
with them laws to set you up. You know what they call
them blank warrants they carry around on them?"

"Yeah," said Henry. "Whiskey warrants."

When Henry stood up before the judge in the courtroom in Muskogee, a court that had been established by
the federal government just to deal with violations of the
liquor laws in the so-called Indian Territory and thereby
to lessen the load on the federal court in Fort Smith, he
took his uncle's advice.

"How do you plead?" droned the judge.

Henry took a deep breath. He steeled himself against
what he was about to do that went so much against his
grain—that so violated his strong sense of *duyukduh.*

"Guilty," he said. He felt cold and hard. He felt betrayed all over again, and most of all he felt as if he had finally, through experience, learned the absolute truth about the white man and his government. The extent of the corruption of the federal law enforcement system, including the courts, had been laid bare before him. He felt smug, and he felt totally cynical.

"The fine is one hundred dollars. Pay the clerk."

The judge rapped his gavel. He was shuffling papers on his desk, pushing those for Henry's case aside and already looking at those for his next victim. He had not once, throughout the entire proceedings, even looked at Henry. Henry turned to walk back to the clerk's table with a smirk on his face. He knew these people, he thought, much better than they knew him. They would not catch him napping again.

"Next case," droned the judge.

Uncle Charlie Starr paid the fine, then he bought Henry a railroad ticket back to Nowata. Henry had a vague feeling that his uncle had been glad to see him off on the train. In fact, Henry thought that there was more than an even chance that Charlie hadn't believed his story this time. He was developing a reputation not of his own making, and the prediction of his dream, the dream in which his friends and relatives had turned their backs on him in shame, was beginning to come true.

9

Back at work at the Todd Ranch, Henry found himself stretching the new barbed wire, which someone else had been required to haul back to the ranch, with another cowboy, named Milo. Milo was about Henry's age, and, like most of the cowboys in that part of the Nation, white. He was likable enough, Henry thought, though not particularly bright—a little slow on the uptake. The day was hot and the work was hard and tedious. Henry would much rather have been working with cows, branding and roping, rounding them up, herding, castrating bulls even, almost anything other than stringing wire. Stringing wire didn't even seem to Henry like cowboy's work. He didn't like the new wire anyway, with its vicious barbs that could rip the flesh of a cow or horse—or a man. He had heard that a white man in Illinois had invented the wire, and that there was a dispute up there over just who actually owned the patent—who was the actual inventor. Henry thought that only a white man could have come up with an idea as wicked as barbed wire, and only a white man would claim another's invention for his own and wind up in court over the whole thing. He banged a staple into the post at which he was working, then sat back heavily on the ground and pulled the bandanna out of his rear pocket to wipe the sweat from his face.

"Milo," he said.

"Yeah?"

"Let's take a breather."

"Yeah," said Milo, moving over to sit beside Henry, "I can use one."

Henry lay back in the dirt with a thoughtful expression on his face.

"Milo," he said, "what are you going to do with your life?"

Milo looked at Henry, his face wrinkled in puzzlement.

"What?" he said.

"You going to break your back like this for somebody else all your life? Sweating in the sun? Eating dust? Stringing this bob wire and tearing your gloves up? Cutting your hands? Getting blisters?"

"Well," said Milo, "I don't intend to work here forever."

"Where are you going then? Some other ranch? One ranch is about like another," said Henry, and he felt something sinister welling up inside him. "What are you going to do?"

"Aw, I don't know. Hell, I—"

"Milo," Henry interrupted, "would you be interested in making some easy money?"

Milo leaned forward. He had taken the bait. Henry didn't dislike Milo. In fact, he kind of liked him in spite of Milo's slow wit. He wasn't really much good for conversation for a man like Henry who, in spite of his lack of formal education, had been a voracious reader for as long as he could remember. But the main thought in Henry's mind, other than the desire to accomplish his immediate goal, was the irony of what he had in mind. It was white people who had spoiled the Cherokee Nation and were ruining Henry's life, and here he was about to lead a white man off the straight and narrow path.

"What have you got in mind, Henry?" said Milo.

"I've been to jail twice, Milo," said Henry, "and the last time I even pled guilty and paid a fine, and I've never committed a crime in my life."

"That's rotten luck, Henry."

"I got to thinking," said Henry, "if I'm going to carry the name of criminal, I might as well be one."

Henry paused to let that last soak in. Milo took off his hat and scratched his head. He had an idea what Henry was leading up to, and he was sort of mulling it over. He waited for Henry to say more, but Henry kept quiet. Finally Milo broke the silence.

"So what have you got in mind?" he asked.

"I was in Nowata at the depot just watching the train come in," said Henry, knowing that he had Milo hooked, "and I noticed a fat roll of bills in the safe. I thought I might make good my bad reputation by robbing that safe. It's an easy job. The depot is open until ten o'clock at night, and the agent's there all by himself. What do you say? You with me?"

Nightfall found the two young cowboys just outside of Nowata looking down onto the town. Both had six-guns tucked into their belts. Milo looked nervous.

"You okay, Milo?" Henry asked.

"Yeah."

"You ready to go through with this? You sure?"

"Yeah. Yeah, I'm ready. I'm okay."

"Then let's go," said Henry, spurring his mount.

Milo followed, and the two rode hard down into the main street of Nowata. No one paid much attention to them. It wasn't unusual for young, rowdy cowboys to ride a little too fast through the streets. Henry led the way to the stockyards and pulled in the reins. He dismounted and tied his horse to a fence rail. Milo did the same. Then Henry looked carefully up and down the street. No one was near, and he pulled a bandanna out of his pocket and tied it around his face. Milo pulled out his own handkerchief, wiped his brow, then tied it over his face.

Quickly the two walked the short distance to the depot.

Henry burst through the door, his six-gun held ready. Milo was right behind him. The agent sat bolt upright and held up his hands. Henry gestured toward the money in the safe, and the agent handed it over. Then the two robbers raced back to their horses and mounted up. Not a word had been said. Still Henry led the way. They raced out of the town the same way they had come in, but on the way out, Henry fired a few shots into the air. When they were outside of town, according to an earlier agreement, they rode off in different directions. They would see each other the next day.

Henry rode out onto the prairie. He would go back to the Todd Ranch, put up the horse and saddle, neither of which was his own, slip into the bunkhouse, and go to bed. In the morning he would get up and start the day as on any other day. Milo was to do basically the same thing, but they had separated so as not to be seen coming back at the same time and together. The way Milo was riding would take him a little longer to get back, but Henry decided to make the interim as long as possible. He spurred up his horse to hurry on back.

Suddenly the horse screamed out in the darkness and bucked, throwing Henry to the ground. Henry's breath was knocked out of him, and he lay senseless for a moment. When he recovered enough to sit up and look around him, he could just see the horse disappearing in the darkness. It was too far to walk back. Besides, he couldn't very well return to the ranch without the horse and saddle. He started to stand up, thinking that he would try to follow the horse, but as he did so, he reached out with one hand and felt a wire. He groped along the wire until something pricked his hand.

"Bob wire," he said out loud.

So that was what had happened. The poor animal had run up on the barbed wire. Henry continued to feel along the wire until his hand felt a thick, warm, and sticky substance.

"Blood."

He knew that he couldn't find the wounded and probably crazed animal in the dark. There was no telling what it had done, which direction it had gone in its pain and fear. Henry lay down in the dirt to await daylight. He slept but little, and as soon as the sun began to let a little light onto the prairie, he was on his feet. There was a good deal of blood on the wire and on the ground beneath it. The horse had been cut badly. Henry looked around and saw a trail of blood on the ground. It was easy to follow, and he figured that the horse couldn't possibly go far as badly as he must have been cut.

He began walking, following the gory trail. He hadn't gone far when, topping a slight rise, he spotted a barn ahead. The bleeding horse had headed straight for it. Henry made his way cautiously to the barn. The door was open, and he edged up to it. He heard voices coming from inside the barn. Peering around the corner of the open doorway, he saw two men standing beside the hurt horse.

"I don't know whose horse it is," one man was saying, "but the saddle belongs to Charles Todd. I recognize it. Hell, I used it when I worked for him last year."

"Well," said the other, "I'll take this into town. If Todd knows who had this saddle, then they'll know who robbed the depot. You just as well shoot that horse. He's too far gone."

Henry got away from the barn quickly. How, he wondered, had they put it all together so easily? Then he remembered that the stolen money was in the saddlebags. They could easily have heard about the robbery. They weren't far from town. Because he couldn't think of anything else to do, Henry walked back to the Todd Ranch. It was late in the day by the time he arrived, and there were two deputy United States marshals waiting for him. He shrugged. It was the pattern of his life. It was natural, and this time it was even just and proper. Henry somehow felt good about that. As the deputies approached him, he could see Milo standing off to one side looking nervous and guilty. Henry ignored Milo and hoped that the slow-witted cowboy would have the good sense to just keep quiet. The prospect of jail no longer worried Henry. Jail was easy to get out of. He had done it before—twice.

10

With the charge of armed robbery against him, Henry found himself back in the Fort Smith jail, and this time he went to court. Charlie Starr appeared once more to help his nephew out of trouble, but Henry was getting to be more and more expensive for Charlie. He could see that his uncle was losing his patience. When asked for his plea, Henry answered, "Guilty," and a trial date was set along with a two-hundred-dollar bond. Uncle Charlie paid the two hundred. Henry assured his uncle that he would appear for the trial so that the bond would not be forfeited. He felt really guilty for the first time since his scrapes with the law had begun, not because he was in fact guilty of the robbery, but because he knew, even as he gave his assurances to his uncle, that he was lying. He had no intention of showing up for the sentencing.

When Henry got back in the vicinity of Nowata and the Todd Ranch, he looked up Milo on the cowboy's day off. Milo had not been suspected. It had been known that two men had committed the robbery, but Milo had gotten his horse back in the corral and had managed to slip back into the bunkhouse undetected. Since the stolen money had been discovered in the saddlebags on the cut horse, no one seemed to be too much concerned about the identity of the other robber, and Henry had been mum on that subject.

The two cowboys arranged to meet at a line shack on the Todd Ranch. They knew that the shack was not being used at the time, so it seemed to be a safe choice. Even though Milo was not suspected of involvement in the robbery, Henry thought it prudent for Milo not to be seen with him just yet.

Inside the shack, Milo rolled a cigarette and offered the makings to Henry.

"No thanks, Milo," said Henry. "I never use tobacco."

"You know what folks are saying around Nowata, Henry?" said Milo as he licked his paper and gave Henry a sly look.

"What's that?" said Henry. It was a polite response. He wasn't really interested in what the good citizens of Nowata thought or felt.

"They're saying you won't show up for the trial."

Henry looked at Milo and smiled.

"They're right," he said, and he felt a pang of guilt concerning his uncle.

Milo's face registered surprise.

"You ain't?"

"No," said Henry. "I'd be a fool to show up for sentencing. I'm guilty, and I've already admitted to it. My role in life is cut out for me now, Milo. No more fooling around. I'm an outlaw. Anybody who doesn't know it yet will know it pretty soon."

Milo struck a match on the wall of the line shack and held the flame up to his damp and twisted cigarette. He sucked in the smoke.

"Henry," he said, "you know that old farmer—I can't 'call his name—just south of town?"

"Old white-haired fat man?" said Henry.

"Yeah. That's the one. He was in the barbershop while back allowing that you just might be guilty because, he says, all Indians is just natural-born thieves. I was sitting there waiting my turn. I heard him say it. 'All Indians is just natural-born thieves,' he said. I heard him."

Milo emptied his lungs of smoke with a long sigh and looked at Henry for the effect of this information.

"Well," said Henry, after only a brief pause, "let's help him maintain his position."

"How we going to do that?"

"Milo," said Henry, "you own your own horse and saddle?"

"You know I don't. I have to ride Mr. Todd's horses."

"Well, I seem to recall a couple of pretty nice-looking saddle broncs at that old man's farm."

The early hours of the next day found Henry and Milo riding across the prairie on two newly acquired mounts with fairly decent saddles. By daylight they had reached the small town of Lenapah. Stores were just beginning to open. Henry led the way to a general store on the main street. Milo followed obediently. The store had just opened for the day. There were few people on the street and no customers in the store. The owner was alone, and he had the cash register opened as Henry stepped in through the front door with Milo close on his heels. The storekeeper looked up, expecting to greet an early customer, and he saw the pistol in Henry Starr's hand.

"Just hand me all that stuff you're counting there, and we'll be on our way," said Henry.

The storekeeper didn't say a word. He took all the money from his cash drawer and laid it on the counter. Henry gestured to Milo, who quickly scraped it all up and stuffed it into his pockets. The two outlaws started to go back outside, but Henry hesitated.

"Wait up," he said.

He moved over to a glass case that contained some pistols.

"Come here, mister," he said.

The storekeeper obeyed.

"Let me have those two .45s."

The man removed the revolvers from the case and laid them out on top for Henry.

"I'll need several boxes of shells," said Henry.

The storekeeper turned around and pulled the shells off a shelf against the wall. He put them down beside the .45s. Up on the same wall near the shelf with the shells some new rifles were displayed, and Henry gave them a quick look.

"Put out two of those .38–.56 Winchesters," he said, "and some shells for them."

Again the storekeeper did as he was told. He was nervous, but he was also efficient. He was a man who obviously had no intention of antagonizing a man with a gun.

"How much does all that come to?" asked Henry.

The poor storekeeper was so dumbfounded that he didn't respond immediately, so Henry had to ask again.

"Well, how much? We are in a little bit of a hurry. I think you can understand that."

The storekeeper did some hasty and nervous figuring.

"Let's see," he said. "These is seventeen dollars each. That's thirty-four. And the rifles is forty. Forty and forty is eighty. And then the shells."

"Sounds to me," said Henry, "that it's going to round off at about a hundred and fifty. That sound right to you?"

"Uh, yes. Yes, that's pretty close."

Henry gave Milo a quick glance.

"How much have we got?" he asked.

Milo was as dumbfounded as the storekeeper, but he tucked his pistol into his waistband and reached into the pocket where he had just a minute earlier stuffed the stolen money. He pulled it out, dumped it back onto the counter and, with some little difficulty, counted it.

"We got right at three hundred here," he said.

"Pay the man his hundred and fifty," said Henry.

Outside of town, riding cross-country once more, Henry called out to Milo.

"Milo, remember Carter's Country Store?"

Milo was still feeling stupefied and was sulking just a bit because of it, but he answered Henry's question.

"Yeah," he said, "I know the place."

"Well," said Henry, "I think we better take a run over there and get some more cash. We spent too much back there in Lenapah."

"Well," said the slow-witted Milo, "what the hell did we spend it for anyway?"

"Milo," said Henry, "stealing money is one thing. Buying guns is another."

11

Henry and Milo had, indeed, gone on to Carter's Country Store and robbed the till. They got one hundred and eighty dollars to add to the one fifty left over from the robbery in Lenapah. Milo was still puzzled about why Henry had bothered to pay for the guns and ammunition, and Henry decided that if Milo couldn't understand his little joke, it wouldn't do any good to try to explain it to him. He did decide, however, that having stolen two horses and robbed two stores, they should probably find someplace to lie low in for a while.

Milo said that he knew a place, and he led Henry to the home of an acquaintance of his known as Frank Cheney. Cheney lived in a small shack on an out-of-the-way road. Henry wondered if Cheney was a renter or just a squatter, but he mentally shrugged it off. Whatever Cheney was, he was obviously not a working farmer, or if he was, he was a very poor one. The place had the look of total neglect. Cheney had broken out a bottle of whiskey, and he and Milo had begun to indulge right away. Henry did not drink (he hadn't lied to the two lawmen who had arrested him for possessing whiskey), and he soon tired of the company of the two carousers. He told Milo and Cheney that he would see them later, cautioned Milo to stay at Cheney's until he got back, then rode off alone.

Henry had only one place to go. It would be just a matter of time before he was known to be the robber of the two stores, and the old farmer whose horses he had stolen had almost surely already accused him of that theft.

In addition, he was known to have pled guilty at Fort Smith to the charge of holding up the depot at Nowata. He hadn't been back to see Todd since his last arrest, and he had no intention of going back. He would not go back home as long as C. N. Walker was there. Henry had no one except Mae, and even if he had had someone else, it was Mae he was missing. He had an ache for her. He headed his horse in the direction of the Morrisons' rented farm.

Mr. Morrison was out in front of the house, busy splitting logs for the wood stove in the kitchen, and Mrs. Morrison had just stepped out on the front porch to shake out a towel, when Henry came riding into the yard.

"Howdy, Mr. Morrison," called Henry.

Morrison didn't miss a stroke with his ax, but he did manage a reply in between swings. He was not a bad man, thought Henry, for a white man. He wasn't too friendly, but that was just because he was always working, and he didn't seem to have much use for anything but work.

"Climb down out of your saddle, son," he said.

Mrs. Morrison looked over her shoulder toward the front door of the house and hollered.

"Mae," she said, "come on out. You've got a caller."

While Henry climbed down off his horse, he thought to himself, *Good. They haven't heard anything yet.*

Mae came out to meet him.

"Hello, Henry," she said.

"Hi."

"You want to stay to dinner?"

Then she looked toward her mother.

"Is it all right, Mama?"

"Sure," said the mother, "you stay and eat with us, Henry."

Henry smiled.

"All right," he said. "Thank you. I'd like that."

"We're having crawdads," said Mae. "That is, if I can catch any. I was just getting ready to go get them. Now that you're staying to dinner, you can help me."

"That was a pretty clever trick," said Henry. "All right. Let's go get them."

"I'll go get a bucket and a pole. Kill a chicken," said Mae, and she ran off toward a lean-to shack off to the side of the house.

Henry looked around at the chickens clucking and pecking about the house. He turned to Mae's mother for advice.

"Which one?" he asked.

"Oh, it don't much matter," said Mrs. Morrison, looking around the yard. "That one on the fence is as good as any."

Henry followed her gaze to a scrawny hen on a fence post about twenty feet to his right. He pulled out his new .45, cocked and aimed it, and squeezed the trigger. There was a loud blast, and the hen's head seemed to explode. The Morrisons' old hound dog set up a howl, which lasted for only a minute. He hadn't bothered to stand up while he was howling. Mae came back with a bucket, a cane pole with a line on it, and a small net. She dropped these items to the ground beside Henry and ran to retrieve the wretched hen, which she soon had plucked in record time. Then she tossed the remains into the bucket.

"I'm ready," she said.

Henry mounted up, then helped Mae to climb up behind him. She carried the bucket, pole and net, and they rode off toward the creek. When they reached a spot where the water ran clear over a bed of flat rocks, they dismounted. Henry allowed the reins of his mount to trail. They sat down by the creek, and Henry pulled apart the carcass of the unfortunate chicken, then tied a piece of the fresh meat to the line on the cane pole.

"You want to wade or fish?" he asked Mae.

"Give me the pole," she said.

Mae took the pole and went to the edge of the water. Reaching out, she lowered the piece of chicken down into the water and onto the flat rocks. Henry pulled off his boots and socks and rolled up the legs of his trousers. He picked up the small net and walked gingerly to the edge of the water to watch the crawdads come crawling out from under the rocks and onto the fresh meat. When the bait was in danger of being overcrowded and the prey was thoroughly absorbed in devouring the raw flesh, Henry went slowly and carefully into the water. He took the line in his right hand and began to ease the bait, still covered with the greedy crawdads, up off the rocks. At the same time, with his left hand, he lowered the net into the water and slipped it under the whole mess. In one scoop they had captured a dozen of the little creatures. In a few hours the bucket was nearly full.

"How's that look?" said Henry.

"Any more and they'll crawl out on top of each other."

They rode back to the house and spent the next while cleaning their catch. Henry was fascinated with the way in which Mae deftly snapped off the heads and cleaned out the small gut with one flick of her thumb. The job was done in time for Mae and Mrs. Morrison to get a great platter of fried crawdads prepared for the dinner table. It was an old Cherokee delicacy that the whites living among the Cherokees had learned about. Mr. Morrison was certainly enjoying the meal. Henry was amused at the way in which the tiny crawdad legs occasionally became tangled in the whiskers of Morrison's moustache. Henry, too, enjoyed the meal and the company, but he felt a little uneasy—a bit anxious or nervous somehow.

Later, outside, the sun low in the sky, Henry knew that he would soon have to take his leave of Mae. His belly was full, and he felt good, but his thoughts were on the future. He took Mae's hand in his.

"Mae," he said, "I've got to tell you something. You're going to hear about it sooner or later anyhow. I'm not working for Mr. Todd anymore."

Henry paused, but Mae didn't respond, so he continued.

"I'm on the scout, Mae. They made me an outlaw."

"Henry," said Mae, "what have you done?"

"I got me a partner, and we stole two horses and robbed two stores. I'm going to get enough money together to get out of this country. There's nothing here for me anymore. Nothing except you. If you'll still have me."

Mae turned and stared off toward the sunset.

"Will you go with me?" said Henry.

Mae turned back to Henry and put her arms around him, pulling him close to her. Henry thrilled at the closeness of her.

"You let me know when you're ready," she said, "and I'll go with you."

They kissed, a brief, tender kiss for fear of the parents' eyes, and Henry went to his horse. He climbed into the saddle.

"I'll be in touch," he said, then he turned the horse and rode away.

He was on his way back to Frank Cheney's house, having stayed late and then ridden the rest of the night away, and it was about midmorning. The road passed close by a ranch house, and Henry noticed several men standing around in front of the house as he approached it. One of the men suddenly pointed in his direction, and Henry heard him shout.

"Hell, that's him right there," said the man. "That's the man you're looking for."

Two of the men in the crowd ran for their horses, mounted up and raced for the road. Henry had not yet come up beside the house, so the two riders, in effect, blocked his path. Then, without a word of warning, one of the riders drew a pistol and fired a shot at Henry. The shot went wild, and Henry dismounted. Pulling his pistol and taking careful aim, he fired. The slug from Henry's .45 hit its mark, and the man was flung backward into the dirt. Henry's horse neighed, shied, and ran off back down the road in the direction from which they had come. The second man, who had ridden out to the road to block Henry's passage, dropped to his belly in the dirt and covered his head with both hands. Henry glanced back toward the ranch house. The rest of the men were just standing there, watching.

Henry kept his gun in hand and walked on down the road until he came to the two men in the dirt, their horses milling around their prostrate figures. He walked up first to the one playing possum, made an audible scoffing snort, then turned to the other. He shoved his six-gun into his waistband, took one of the loose horses by the reins, mounted up, and rode on his way. No one followed, and soon he had left the ranch house behind. No one followed, but he had killed a man. Now there would be no turning back. As he made his way on down the road, he wondered who the man was he had just killed. He had never before killed a man, and he didn't particularly like the feeling. He figured that the two must have been lawmen, and he thought of all his previous experiences with that bunch. Well, he wasn't going to lose any sleep over that fellow, whoever he was. The man had shot first and with no warning. He had gotten just what he asked for—just what he deserved. Henry hoped that the man was a deputy United States marshal.

12

The dead man was a railroad detective and a former deputy United States marshal. Although Henry had no way of knowing that at the time he killed the man, the incident certainly increased the desire of the authorities to apprehend the young Indian outlaw. A reward of twelve hundred dollars was offered for his capture. In turn, the killing and the reward further strengthened Henry's own conviction that there could be no other life for him in this world than that of a hunted criminal.

He led Frank Cheney on a lightning raid of Chouteau. They rode into town, went into the general store and held it up, then, with guns still drawn, walked outside and across the street to a second store. They held it up, still with no interference from anyone, moved on to the M.K. & T. railroad depot, and cleaned that establishment out of cash on hand. Milo did not accompany Henry and Frank Cheney on that expedition. Henry thought that it was best for Milo to stay behind. He had become nervous. He wouldn't be reliable. He was back at Cheney's place, drunk.

Not long after the raid on Chouteau, Henry and Frank robbed a store at Inola. By this time deputies were riding in pairs throughout the Cherokee Nation in search of Henry Starr and whoever might be with him. He had become a high priority on their list. They wanted him badly. More significantly, Isaac Parker wanted him badly in his courtroom, and when Parker wanted someone, the pressure was on the deputies.

But Henry had his supporters as well. Inside a barn not far from Nowata, a country band of locals was making music. The band, like the crowd out on the "dance floor," was a mixture of Indian and white. An old-fashioned barn dance or country hoedown was in progress. People came and went on their own time to and from these affairs, so a late arrival was nothing to marvel at, but when the door opened and a young Indian man came in with a young white girl, the music stopped. All eyes turned toward the latecomers. It was not the fact that one was white and the other was Indian. There were several such couples already in attendance, and that was a common enough occurrence in the Cherokee Nation in those times, though many would have been more comfortable had the sex roles been reversed. No, it was something else that astonished the merrymakers. The silence was finally broken by a white farmer.

"It's Henry Starr," he shouted.

That announcement was followed by another brief moment of awkward silence.

"There's twelve hundred dollars on his head," said another, though not quite as loudly as the first had spoken. This comment, too, was followed by strained silence. Then an old woman stepped boldly out toward the center of the room.

"Well," she said in a confident and commanding voice, "some of you boys go on outside and keep a watch so's Henry and his girl can have a good time here and not have to be aworrying about is the laws coming."

Two husky young country ruffians obeyed, and Henry gave the lady a nod.

"Thank you, ma'am," he said. Then he addressed the whole crowd. "Well, don't let my entrance stop the music."

The fiddler, an Indian, struck up a lively reel and was quickly joined by the rest of the band. Several couples began to dance as Henry led Mae to the refreshment table. A few moved to greet Henry Starr and shake his hand while others clustered in small groups to whisper about the celebrity in their midst.

A white farmer leaned over confidentially to an old Indian man standing next to him back against the wall.

"They say he wears a steel breastplate to stop bullets," he said.

The old Indian responded, a twinkle in his eye, but his expression otherwise totally somber.

"I know he does for a fact," he said. "I seen it once."

There was a third man standing by who could no longer keep himself out of this conversation. He stepped in between the other two, as the white farmer was still nodding, happy to have had his information confirmed.

"A dead shot, too," said the newcomer. "I once seen him cut a fence wire with one shot from thirty yards off."

Before the evening was done and Henry had to take Mae home, he had not only danced with Mae, but also with nearly every other female present, both young and old, and he had stepped up onto the bales of hay that served as a bandstand and played a few tunes on the fiddle. All in all it had turned out to be a very satisfactory evening, and Henry was sorry to see it come to an end.

Out in the woods and on the prairies the deputy marshals continued their search.

It was in the early hours of the morning, after the dance had ended and Henry Starr had taken Mae Morrison safely home to her parents, that he was riding alone back toward the shack of Frank Cheney, which had begun to serve as his outlaw headquarters. He thought about his new role of outlaw celebrity, and he liked it. He liked the attention and the admiration of the country folks, both Indian and white, and he despised the deputy marshals and was enjoying making fools of them. He also thought about Mae and his claim that he was only getting enough money together to take them out of this part of the country to someplace where they could start over together. Henry was walking his horse casually down a country road and thinking these thoughts when he heard the distinct sound of a buggy approaching from up ahead. He moved over to the side of the road, halted his pony, and dismounted. Letting the reins trail on the ground, he drew his pistols and waited. When the buggy came closer, he could see two men riding in it. There were no badges showing, but to Henry, the men had the look of deputies. They hadn't spotted him yet when he called out from the darkness there beside the road.

"Hold up there," he said.

The startled driver jerked the reins and stopped the buggy. Both men froze.

"Laws, is it?" said Henry. "You fellows must be looking for me."

"Why," said the buggy's passenger in a quavering voice, "who are you?"

Henry stepped out farther into the road, holding his six-guns out prominently.

"Now, that's a terrible blow to my ego, mister," he said, "but I'll just figure that it's on account of the darkness that you couldn't recognize such a famous guy as I am."

The buggy driver, without turning his head, leaned slightly toward his partner.

"It's Henry Starr," he said in a low voice.

The other spoke up loudly.

"Hey, don't kill us," he said. "We ain't even after you. Honest."

"What else would you be doing out in these parts tonight?" demanded Henry, and he thought what a bunch of cowards these deputies were.

"Uh, whiskey warrants, Mr. Starr," stammered the

driver, revealing to Henry that, indeed, the two were deputy marshals. "Whiskey warrants. That's all. I swear it."

Henry took another step forward and addressed his
next question to the passenger.

"Is that right?"

"Yes, sir. That's all we're doing. We wasn't even thinking of you."

Henry's experience with deputies had taught him to
despise all of their kind, and the groveling, the apparent
cowardliness of these two made him despise them all the
more. They were brave enough when they encountered
an unarmed and unsuspecting boy, but out here in the
dark, facing his guns, they showed their true colors, he
thought. Still, he could not shoot down helpless men. It
just was not in his nature.

"You know," he said, "it was one of you dirty skunks
with a whiskey warrant that railroaded me when I was an
innocent, law-abiding citizen and set me on the path to
this life of crime. I ought to blow both of you off of that
wagon, but you're not worth the price of the bullets. Now
get out of here before I change my mind and decide to do
it anyway."

He fired a shot over their heads, and the buggy bolted
forward as if the shot had started it. Henry didn't have to
stand and watch after it for long. It was soon out of sight.
He shoved his pistols back into his waistband and went
back to his horse. Mounting up, he continued on his way.

Not far down the road, in the light of a dim moon in
the west, Henry saw ahead of him the outlines of a small
village. It was one of those out-of-the-way Cherokee settle-
ments that somehow never show up on the maps. Henry
knew the place, but he rode cautiously down the road. A
dog barked. Soon others joined him. There were no other
sounds than the barking. Henry urged his horse on
through the jumble of log cabins and frame shacks. Suddenly an old woman seemed to materialize in a doorway

just to Henry's left. Her appearance seemingly out of nowhere startled him just a bit.

" *'Siyo,* " she said, her gravelly voice seeming uncommonly loud in the still night.

"*Osiyo,* " said Henry, returning her greeting. "*Tohiju?*"

"*Osd',* " said the old one. Then shifting to English, she continued, "Be careful where you ride tonight. They are all over the damn place."

Henry smiled and tipped his hat.

"*Wado,* little grandmother," he said, and the woman seemed to vanish as mysteriously as she had appeared.

The dogs continued to bark as Henry nudged his pony into a slow forward gait. When he reached the edge of the settlement, Henry stopped. He saw nothing ahead of him, but he had an unexplainable sense of foreboding, fed by the old woman's eerie warning. A few dogs still barked occasionally behind him. Henry dismounted and pulled his Winchester out of its saddle carriage. He cranked a shell into the chamber, and the noise of the lever action seemed to resound in the stillness. He sat motionless in the saddle for a moment, the rifle ready, and surveyed the scene ahead of him. Not too far from where he waited, a lane wound in to the road from the right just ahead of a small farmhouse. To the left of the road was nothing but open prairie. The thing that captured Henry's attention was the lane. He led his horse off the road and tied it to a small tree, then eased himself on foot on down closer to the lane.

Within about ten feet of the intersection, he stopped and waited. For a few seconds more, the silence reigned, then he heard the sound of approaching horses. Soon two riders came into his view on the lane, riding toward the road. As they were about to enter the road, and so were nearly abreast of Henry, he made his presence known to them.

"Keep riding straight ahead," he commanded, "or I'll blast your souls into eternal damnation."

Almost as a unit, the two horses and two riders hesitated an instant, then shot forward across the road and into the prairie on the other side. Henry stepped into the road and shouted after them.

"I'm Henry Starr, and I'm a dead shot."

He watched them disappear into the darkness and listened as the noise of their horses' hooves faded away in the distance, then he went back to where he had left his own pony. Once more he mounted up and headed on his way. He had ridden another mile or so when he saw three riders come up out of a gulley in the distance ahead. It was too far for a pistol shot. This time the riders and Henry spotted each other almost simultaneously. Knowing that he had been seen, Henry jerked the rifle from its scabbard as he dismounted, then dropped to the ground flat on his belly. Looking forward, he saw the three riders dismount and stand by their horses. He waited for them to make a move, but they made none. He finally decided to break the silence.

"Hey, over there," he shouted. "I'm Henry Starr. I just ran off your two buddies down the road there."

He waited for a response, but none came. The three men stood silently beside their horses in the moonlight.

"If you're looking for that twelve hundred that's on my head," he called out to them, "I'm ready to fight you to the end."

He could see the three move their heads, looking at one another. Still they made no reply.

"If you don't have the stomach for a fight," shouted Henry, running out of patience, "then back off now while you have the chance. Otherwise I'll blow you off the prairie."

The three silhouettes began to mill around some, then, apparently accepting the offer Henry had made, they began to back away slowly, leading their horses. After a few backward steps they mounted up and rode off at a fast clip. Henry heaved a sigh of relief and got to his feet. Satisfied that these latest three minions of the law at Fort Smith had left, he resumed his journey. This time, however, he decided to leave the road. He trotted his pony a space across the prairie until he came to a wire fence, reached into his saddlebags for a pair of wire cutters, snipped the wires, and rode out across a wheat field at a gallop. He had seen enough deputy United States marshals for one night.

"Little grandmother was right," he said. "They are all over the damn place."

13

Back at Cheney's farmhouse, Henry found Cheney and Milo sitting on the porch. Milo was sagging in a cane-bottom chair and looked to be in pretty bad shape. He had been drinking hard and steadily for some time but had recently run out of liquor. His clothes were dirty and rumpled, and his hair was tousled. As Henry rode up to the house, Cheney came down off the porch to meet him.

"They're all over the countryside," said Henry. "I ran five of them off last night without firing a shot."

"They're a bunch of cowards," said Frank. "They won't fight a man fair. I ain't never heard of one of them fighting a man fair. Only if they can ambush you."

Milo stirred in his chair and moaned.

"There's too many of them," he said, his voice a high-pitched whine.

"Yeah," Frank agreed. "They've even been nosing around here."

"Henry, I think you better get out of the country," said Milo. "Your trail's getting too hot."

Henry pulled the saddle off his horse and heaved it over the porch rail. He put one foot up on the porch and leaned with his elbow on his knee.

"Well, Milo," he said, "if my trail's getting too hot for you, maybe you better go where you can cool your heels. I'm staying right here."

"There won't be no hard feelings?" whimpered Milo.

"No hard feelings," said Henry, leading his horse

around to the small corral beside the house. "We'll be seeing you around, Milo."

"Yeah, well, so long, boys," said Milo, getting up off his chair. He hurried inside and reappeared a moment later with a saddle roll. On his way to the corral, he passed Henry, who was returning to the house. As he did, he walked sideways so he could keep his eyes on Henry. Apparently Milo wasn't quite certain that Henry had told him the truth when he had said that there'd be no hard feelings. Milo took his own saddle off the fence rail and saddled his horse. He mounted up clumsily and rode off without another word.

Henry Starr took the dipper off its hook on the porch and dipped it into the water barrel. He took a long drink and spat. The water was stale. He leaned on a post and stared after the fleeing Milo. Cheney had returned to his chair. Henry wondered if Milo would go back to being an honest cowboy or continue on the outlaw trail somewhere else, on his own or with someone else. It didn't really matter. He didn't belong in this Cherokee country anyway.

As Milo disappeared, Henry's thoughts returned to the deputies he had encountered the night before. They must really want him bad, he thought, and for what? Robbing a few country stores? Killing that coward who had shot first and with no warning? That, as Henry saw it, had been self-defense. It didn't seem worth it somehow. That is, what he had done didn't seem to him to merit all the attention he was getting from the deputies. Things were all out of proportion—out of balance. Well, he would fix that.

He spoke to Frank Cheney without turning around. "Frank, I've got something on my mind."

"What's that?" asked Cheney.

"The Caney Valley National Bank in Caney, Kansas."

Cheney leaned forward in his chair, his elbows on his

knees. He raised his eyebrows and looked intently at Henry.

"We going to rob it?" he said.

"That's my intention, Frank," said Henry. "We're about to graduate to the next level of outlawry."

14

Henry Starr and Frank Cheney rode at a comfortable pace toward Caney, Kansas. They rode common cow ponies, but they were leading two fine thoroughbreds, which they had obtained just for this occasion at the small cost of only a couple of hours of their time. Each man carried two .45 Colt pistols and two Winchester rifles. They were only a little way out of Caney when Henry selected a spot beside the road. They led the thoroughbreds off into a clump of trees and tied them, then moved on toward Caney.

It began to drizzle. Henry called another halt. They dismounted, wrapped the four rifles to protect them from the rain, and hid them beside the road. Then they rode on into Caney, making their entrance by a back street. They hitched the cow ponies. Henry looked at Frank, gave a nod, and they walked off in different directions. Circling the block, the two men met at the front door of the Caney Valley National Bank. They did not acknowledge each other. Henry opened the door and stepped inside, standing against the wall, the rainwater running off the brim of his hat. Frank Cheney passed him by and walked to the teller's window. Henry made a quick survey of the situation inside the bank.

There were two cashiers and a bank officer behind the wicket and two customers at the counter. Frank, standing behind one of the customers, looked over his shoulder at Henry, who gave him a nod. Both men drew their pistols at once, and one of the cashiers bolted into the large vault.

The officer ran through a door into a back room. Henry, reacting quickly, made for the latter, and poked the barrel of one six-shooter in between the door and the door-facing just in time to prevent the officer from closing the door after himself. Henry pushed the door on open to find the man reaching for a rifle that was standing in a corner of the back room. Henry stepped into the room and shoved his two pistols menacingly toward the banker, who responded appropriately by freezing in position with his right arm extended toward the rifle. Henry gestured with one six-gun toward the main room, and the banker obediently went back out behind the cage. Frank had corraled the teller who had run into the vault. Frank was watching the whole crowd and awaiting Henry's return.

As Henry took over the job of watching the crowd and gave a nod, Frank Cheney pulled a two-bushel sack out of the waistband of his trousers.

"I've kept this sack on my farm seven years," he said, "just for this purpose."

He stepped inside the vault with the sack. Henry, keeping one pistol pointed toward the crowd, moved behind the counter and began to gather up the bills from off the counter and from the tellers' drawers. A customer approached the front door, and Henry quickly whipped off his hat and used it to cover his weapon on the counter. The customer stepped inside and turned his back for an instant to shut the door behind him. Henry moved the hat over, so that when the man turned again, he found himself staring at Henry's Colt.

"Just come on over here with the others," said Henry.

The man did as he was told, and just then Frank came out of the vault with his sack about two-thirds full. He saw the money Henry had gathered up on the counter and moved to add it to his collection. Henry went to a back door and opened it to see where it led. He found a high stockade-type fence enclosing a small area behind the bank and allowing no exit into the alley. Leaving the door open, he turned back to the crowd in the bank.

"All right," he said. "Everyone out. Right through here."

"Get going," said Frank.

The three bank employees and three customers were hustled out the back door into the small enclosure, and Henry pulled the door shut and latched it from the inside. He made a quick side trip into the back room and picked up the banker's rifle, then moved to the front door, where Frank was waiting for him. They gave each other a look, then Frank opened the door and began walking toward the end of the block. Henry followed, holding the rifle ready for action. A few onlookers on the sidewalks paused to watch curiously, but no one made a move toward the two bank robbers. When Henry rounded the corner to walk on to where they had left their horses, Frank already had the animals untied. They mounted up and started for the edge of town at a gallop.

Once out of town, they spurred the mounts and raced full-speed down the road. Soon they reached the spot where the rifles were cached, and they pulled their cow ponies to a halt. Frank moved to uncover the rifles, while Henry took the banker's rifle by the barrel and smashed it over a rock. Taking up their own extra rifles, they mounted up again. After a quick glance back toward town, the fugitives continued their ride. A few men had mounted horses back in Caney and were starting their pursuit.

Henry, with Frank following, spurred his pony toward a scrub oak-covered knoll just ahead but off the road. As they topped the rise, they disappeared into the shadows of the scrub oaks from the view of their pursuers. Riding down the other side of the knoll, Henry led Frank in a sharp turn to the right, heading back for the road. The makeshift posse from Caney followed in hot pursuit over the knoll and through the scrub oaks, but then continued straight ahead. Henry's ruse had worked.

Back on the road, it wasn't long before Henry and Frank came back to the spot where they had hidden the two thoroughbred horses. They dismounted, unsaddled and turned loose the worn-out cow ponies, threw the saddles on the fresh mounts and continued on their way at a leisurely pace, joking and laughing with each other at the ease with which they had evaded those Kansas hicks.

Later, back at Cheney's farmhouse, they emptied the contents of the sack onto a table. Cheney marveled at the pile of money in front of him.

"There must be fifty thousand dollars there," he said.

Henry said nothing. He sat down and started counting. He had noticed something that bothered him. Frank, still eager, decided to lend a helping hand, and when the count was finished, Henry leaned back in his chair as he tossed down the final stack of bills.

"Four thousand nine hundred," he said.

"Damn," said Frank, scratching his head. "That's all?"

"It's all small bills," said Henry. "They foxed us, Frank."

Henry chuckled. He enjoyed a good joke, even when it was on him. He had planned the robbery carefully with the extra horses and rifles. In fact, he mused, if anything, he had overplanned. The extra rifles had been totally superfluous, and so might have been the thoroughbred horses. Even though he had planned every move, the sly bankers had somehow secreted all the big bills. When he had relished the humor in the bankers' trick and stopped chuckling at himself, Henry sat for a moment in silence. Frank hadn't seen the humor in the small bills, but he could see that Henry was in deep thought, so he kept quiet and waited. Finally Henry spoke again.

"There's too many people in a bank," he said. "We can't watch them all—just the two of us. Frank, if we're going to be successful in this business, we've got to go about it the right way. What we need is a band of outlaws."

15

Henry Starr and Frank Cheney sat up late discussing possibilities for recruits into their gang, and early the following morning they rode out together, Cheney, for a change, taking the lead. They rode up to within view of a shabby farm. Cheney had guided Henry to this place. They stopped to survey the scene before them. The farm was generally run-down. The small house needed painting, but before that could be done, it needed some other, more basic, repairs. Tall weeds grew all around, and the fence had fallen down in several spots.

A man of about thirty-five, with a sallow complexion, watery blue eyes, and dark brown hair, was drawing water from a well with a rusty and squeaking pulley. Although Starr and Cheney were not far off, the man had obviously either not seen them or was purposely not letting on that he had. He went about his task seemingly unconcerned. After taking in the scene, the two riders urged their mounts on into the farmyard, Cheney still in the lead. The man set the bucket down and reached for a nearby rifle. The rifle, too, showed signs of being ill cared for. As Henry Starr rode in closer, he thought to himself, *Squatter.* When they got well into the yard, the man lowered his rifle.

"Hello, Frank," he said.

Cheney nodded.

"Watt," he said, "I want you to meet Henry Starr."

"Henry Starr?" said Watt.

"That's right," said Henry. "The outlaw."

"We'd like to talk to you, Watt," said Cheney.

Watt glanced toward the house. The front door swung open, and a wretched, washed-out-looking woman stepped out. Her skin, hair, and dress all seemed to have been made out of the same basic gray material. She looked with curiosity toward the men.

"Not here," said Watt, and he started walking toward a barn that looked as if it were leaning about as far to one side as it could without falling over. Henry and Frank followed him. So did the woman's gaze. She wondered what the men were talking about. She could see them out by the barn, but she could not hear anything they might be saying. The two strangers still sat on their horses. Watt stood on the ground before them. Soon Watt turned and walked into the barn.

"Watt?" the woman called out. "Watt?"

Watt did not respond, and the woman did not move away from the house. She stood straining her eyes toward the two horsemen and the barn. Soon Watt emerged from the barn leading a horse, saddled. When he had gotten back to where the others sat horseback waiting for him, he climbed into the saddle.

"Watt," the woman cried.

The three riders turned their mounts and started toward the road. Only then did the woman move. She took three hurried steps toward the riders, wringing her hands.

"Where are you going?" she said. "Watt?"

Henry Starr's recruiting process had begun. The three rode back to Cheney's place, where Henry gave the other two instructions to practice shooting. They set bottles and cans up on the fence posts and fired at them. If he was going to lead an outlaw gang, Henry decided, they would have to be good. Their lives would, after all, depend on each other.

Henry left the two at Cheney's and went off alone.

Frank and Watt waited for two days for Henry to return, and, now and then, according to Henry's instructions, they would set up their bottles and cans and shoot. They were engaged in this process when they heard riders approaching. They turned, guns ready. Three riders came into the yard, but Frank and Watt put away their pistols when they recognized that Henry Starr was in the lead.

"Boys," said Henry, "meet Link Cumplin and Happy Jack."

The strength of Henry Starr's gang was now at five, but he was not yet satisfied. He left them all to practice their shooting and continued to scout the countryside for more recruits. Another week passed, and the four began to grow restless. They had done nothing but shoot, until Henry had added a riding drill to their daily routine. They practiced riding in a line, like a cavalry charge. They practiced riding by the targets on the fence posts and shooting at them from horseback at a full gallop. Link Cumplin said that he could have joined the army for this, but Henry assured him that the pay would be better. He also assured them all that soon they would see some action and some profit. The main thing, he said, was that in order for this scheme to work, they all had to agree to accept his decisions without question. He had to be the boss of the outfit.

One day not long after that, Henry took them all out on a practice ride. They rode abreast across country when the country would allow that formation. When the woods grew thick and they had to keep to the road, they shifted to single file. The men had no idea where they were going. As far as they knew, Henry was just putting them through the motions once again, so they were a little surprised when he led them into the small town of Coweta and halted at a hitching rail across the street from the jail. They all dismounted and hitched their horses, then leaned against the rail waiting—for what, no one knew but Henry Starr.

Across the street, inside the jail, the sheriff unlocked the cell door and motioned to the prisoner who was lounging inside on the cot.

"All right, Tyler," he said. "Come on out."

The man called Tyler roused himself up from the cot in the cell, put his hat on his head, hitched his trousers up, and walked out of the cell with a swagger. The sheriff walked around behind his desk and opened up a drawer. He pulled an envelope out of the drawer and tossed it across the desk at Tyler.

"Here's your things," he said.

"What about my horse and saddle?" asked Tyler.

"Just outside," said the sheriff. "I had him brought up from the livery. You're free to go now. Take my advice and watch your step."

"See you around," said Tyler as he stepped to the door and opened it.

"I hope not," said the sheriff.

Tyler shut the door behind himself, and the sheriff heard a voice shout from somewhere outside.

"Bud Tyler," it said.

The sheriff got up from his chair and moved to the window. Looking outside, he could see five men, real hardcases, he thought, lined up at the hitching rail across the street. He watched as Tyler untied his horse and ambled across the street to meet the others. He had a brief conversation with one of the men, an Indian by his looks, then mounted up with the rest of them and rode out of town.

"God damn," said the sheriff, walking heavily back to his chair.

Now they were six. Tyler's was the final name on the list that Starr and Cheney had compiled. Henry was satisfied. Another week or so of training to get Tyler in step with the others, and they'd be ready to go.

It was after dark a few nights later, and the Henry Starr Gang was lounging around inside the cabin of Frank Cheney when they heard something move outside. All eyes looked toward the door. Henry Starr eased a pistol out of a holster and cocked it. The door creaked open, seemingly by itself. Outside was dark, and the men inside could see no one in the doorway. Henry held his pistol ready. There was silence for a few long seconds.

"Step inside and show yourself," said Henry.

A young man about nineteen years old with sandy hair and piercing green eyes stepped to just inside the door. He was short and thin. Henry thought, in fact, that he seemed even slightly anemic in appearance, but hanging from the crossed cartridge belts that he wore around his slim waist were two very large and well-cared-for .45s. The slight stranger's eyes shifted around the room as the men sat up, their eyes all intent on him.

"Which one is Henry Starr?" asked the intruder.

"I have that dubious distinction," said Henry, still holding the cocked pistol. "And who might you be?"

"They call me Kid Wilson. Word's out that you're recruiting. I come to join up with you."

"What do you say, boys?" said Henry.

"I've heard about him," said Happy Jack. "He's all right."

Henry eased the hammer down on his Colt and holstered the weapon. He stood up and offered his hand to Kid Wilson. Wilson took it, and his eyes were fixed on Henry's. Staring into another's eyes made Henry just a bit uncomfortable, but he knew that it was a common practice of whites, so he returned the stare.

"Well," he said, "I think that this will just about fill up our ranks, boys."

Now the number was seven—a good number, Henry thought. To the Cherokees, a sacred number—a number of power. Seven. Himself and six more. And the six were all white. He would not lead an Indian down the path to trouble. Henry thought, with a sense of irony, that here with these six men around him, he was more alone than ever. He had no one except Mae. He would whip this gang into shape, rob a few banks, build up a substantial money roll, and then take Mae and leave the country. And the sooner the better.

He intensified the training, taking on the role of drill instructor. Target practice with both pistol and rifle was every day's business. And he added to their repertoire a riding drill in which the gang formed up in a fan shape, the men on either side firing to the right or left, and those in the center firing straight ahead. They also engaged in fast draw practice.

One day Henry took Bud Tyler with him, leaving the others at Cheney's house. They were all lounging around the front of the house, following some target practice, when Henry rode back into the yard beside a wagon.

"What the hell?" said Link Cumplin, rising to his feet.

Henry and the wagon came on up to the house. Bud Tyler was driving.

"What's that?" said Frank Cheney.

"Gentlemen," said Henry, "this is our chuck and ammunition wagon, fully fitted out. Mr. Tyler is our teamster. Now we are ready to go."

The next morning the Henry Starr Gang started out on its first job. Bud Tyler drove the wagon, and the other six rode along beside it. They made the trip to within a few miles of Pryor Creek, where Henry called a halt. He ordered Bud Tyler to stay with the wagon and wait for them. Henry and the other five headed for the town at a trot.

In Pryor Creek the train was just pulling in, and a crowd had gathered at the depot. Henry Starr rode for the engine. He caught up with it easily, pulled himself from the saddle onto the engine, and stepped inside with the conductor. He pulled out a .45 and leveled it at the man.

"Just ease it on in like nothing's wrong," he said.

At just about the same time, Happy Jack had climbed onto the rear end of the caboose. He pulled out his pistols and started to make his way through the cars from that end, gathering up everyone he came across and herding them in front of him. Outside, the other four remained on horseback and rode up in a semicircle, firing their pistols in the air and herding the crowd like a bunch of cows up toward the train. As the people in the train were pushed toward the center from each end by Happy Jack and Henry, they were forced out to join the general crowd. Soon the train was empty, and Henry and Jack came out into the crowd. They were joined by Link and Watt. Kid Wilson and Frank Cheney remained mounted and held their guns on the crowd. The four outlaws down in the midst of the crowd pulled sacks out of their waistbands and began taking up a collection. As he moved through the crowd, Henry spotted two deputy United States marshals. He took particular delight in disarming them. The deputies, for their part, made no move to resist. Typical, Henry thought. Now and then Kid Wilson and Frank Cheney would fire a shot or two into the air to keep the crowd suitably intimidated.

The sacks full, the pockets of the crowd all empty, Henry made a flourishing gesture, and the four outlaws on foot all headed for their horses. Henry had to jump back through the engine to retrieve his mount. He climbed into the saddle and rode around the train to rejoin the rest of the gang, and as he did so, he saw Happy Jack riding from the rear of the train, having accomplished the same purpose. With everyone ready to go,

Henry turned in his saddle to face the crowd one last time.

"Just so there'll be no mistakes, I'm Henry Starr, folks," he shouted. "See you later."

He spurred his horse and headed out of Pryor Creek in the direction of Bud Tyler and the wagon with the rest of the Starr Gang following. They made it back to the wagon with no problems. Kid Wilson dropped back occasionally to check the back trail. No one from Pryor Creek followed, and Wilson was just a bit disappointed. The gang headed home, each one feeling high on the excitement and the success of their first venture. As they moved along a road at an arrogantly easy pace, they passed a small farm. The farmer, out working in the yard, looked up at the strange caravan. Suddenly he turned toward his house.

"Maw," he shouted. "Maw, come looka here."

A woman came rushing out the front door and ran to the farmer's side. She was followed by several barefoot children.

"That there's Henry Starr and his gang," said the farmer.

"Henry Starr?" said one of the children.

Henry had noticed the family gathering outside of the farmhouse. He turned his head and looked at the farmer and his brood.

"Howdy," shouted the farmer. "Howdy, Henry Starr. You'ns give them hell."

Henry smiled and tipped his hat to the farmer as he rode on past. The farmer and his whole family stood still, as if for a family photographic portrait, and watched the Starr Gang ride on down the road and out of sight. When there was nothing left to watch but the dust, the head of the family spoke again.

"Ain't no way the laws will touch them boys," he said. "Hell, they're too damn scared to try."

16

The Starr Gang with its chuck and ammunition wagon moved along the road heading south. Henry felt good. He had planned carefully, and his plans had met with success. All the rigorous training to which he had subjected his gang had paid off. They were a crack outfit, he thought. Still, he felt alone among them, but that was all right, too. The leader need not, probably should not, be a part of the gang. He should remain separate, apart, aloof. Henry had not forgotten his promise to Mae, his plan to collect enough money for the two of them to go away some-where, but he was enjoying life with the Starr Gang. It was exciting. It was romantic. It even somehow satisfied a vaguely nationalistic feeling that burned somewhere deep in Henry's breast, for he felt that the law that he defied was the law of an invader. Henry kept trying to hate white people, but he kept running across whites he liked —or at least whites he could not really dislike. As he rode along the road with his gang, he realized that he was be-ginning to like one of them. He couldn't really pin down what it was he liked, but there was something about the mysterious Kid Wilson.

Henry called a halt to his caravan.

"Let's rest up here for a spell," he said.

Bud Tyler pulled the wagon off the road, and the riders all dismounted and let the reins of their horses trail on the ground. Henry waited for everyone to stretch and get the riding kinks out, then he called them all together.

"Boys," he said, "we did all right on that job, but I

formed this group for things more serious than that circus back there. I'm talking about banks. Bud, just as soon as we rustle up some chuck and get our bellies full, I want you to head this wagon east. We're going to Bentonville, Arkansas."

Bentonville, Arkansas, in 1893, was a thriving town. It was larger than any of the towns in the Cherokee Nation or in Kansas that Henry had pulled jobs in so far. Bentonville was a busy town with heavy traffic on the streets. Men on horseback, men driving wagons, men and women in buggies, and many pedestrians were coming and going on the main street. Into this bustle the Henry Starr Gang prepared to ride and rob the large and solid-looking bank on Main Street.

From a hilltop just on the outskirts of Bentonville, Henry and his boys looked down on the unsuspecting town. Henry and Frank were in the wagon with Bud Tyler, their horses tied onto the back. The others sat in their saddles. Henry studied the street. He saw the customers coming and going through the front door of the bank. This job would call for all the discipline and precision he had been drilling into his small band of brigands. He gave a nod, and Tyler flicked the reins, starting the wagon down the hill, straight toward Main Street. Kid Wilson and Happy Jack rode as a pair off to the right of the wagon, Link Cumplin and Watt to the left.

In the bank, business went on as usual, while the Starr Gang gathered in a back alley. As soon as the wagon came to a stop, Kid Wilson jumped out of the saddle and ran to the back end of the wagon to pull out the rifles and distribute them to all the gang members. Henry, Wilson, and Cheney, rifles in hand, started for the bank at a trot. Link followed not far behind. They had left Tyler with the wagon, and Happy Jack and Watt to hold the horses ready. As Henry approached the bank, he found the front door open, someone having just gone inside. Before the door could swing to, Henry jumped through into the lobby, followed by Kid Wilson and Frank Cheney. They spread out and leveled their rifles.

"Hands up and hands steady," shouted Henry.

Outside, Link Cumplin had taken a position just by the front door of the bank. He held his rifle ready and watched nervously the chaos of the street. Link should have at least lounged against the wall a bit casually. His posture attracted immediate attention, and the attention that he drew made Link more nervous. He pointed his rifle first in one direction, then in another. With all the people in the street, there was no way that Link could begin to keep track of their comings and goings, and someone had alerted the local sheriff. Bentonville was not like Pryor Creek. The citizens of Bentonville had no intention of allowing their bank to be robbed without putting up a fight. The sheriff, pistol in hand, came running toward the bank through the crowd on the street. Link saw him and threw his rifle to his shoulder, but before he could fire, the sheriff pointed his six-shooter and pulled the trigger.

Inside the bank Frank Cheney and Kid Wilson were busy gathering up money from the cashiers. Henry was keeping the crowd under control. When the shot was fired outside, all three looked toward the door, but before anyone could speak, there were more shots. Kid Wilson shouted.

"What's that?"

"It's Link," said Henry, running to the door. "Hurry it up."

One of the shots from outside crashed through the bank's front window. The crowd in the bank started to panic. Wilson and Cheney grabbed what cash they could and stuffed it into their bags. Henry tried to get a look outside, but the bullets were flying too fast around the door. Link must be cut to pieces, he thought. He had to think fast.

"All right," he said. "Let's go."

Frank Cheney looked incredulous.

"Out there?" he said.

"Yeah. We're taking everybody with us," said Henry, turning his pistols back on the crowd of bank employees and customers. "Come on. You walk ahead of us, and you stay bunched up. Otherwise we'll blast you. You got that? Now get going."

The crowd pushed its way through the front door, but the shooting didn't stop. Link was still standing, but it looked to Henry as if he were being held up by the bullets as they hit him. He was covered with blood and had been hit at least once in the face. It looked to Henry at a glance as if Link's eye had been shot out. In the confusion, some of the hostages began to scatter, ignoring Henry's earlier threat. It was just a threat, for Henry's attention was not on the fleeing hostages, nor had he ever intended shooting any of them, no matter what happened. His attention was on Link and on those who were shooting at them. Henry grabbed Link by one arm.

"Come on," he said.

When the people out in the street, including the sheriff and those who had been shooting with him, saw that Link had been joined by two of his cohorts who were now shooting back at them, they scattered for cover. Henry, dragging Link, and Wilson and Cheney made it around the corner and on over to the horses, where Watt and Happy Jack took Link from Henry and helped the wounded man into his saddle. As soon as Bud Tyler saw that the others had returned, he whipped up the team and started the wagon out of town and across the valley. The horseback riders were not far behind. At the end of Main Street, Henry, Frank Cheney, and Kid Wilson turned their horses to face the town and fired some shots to hold back pursuit and allow the others time to get some distance between themselves and Bentonville. When the others were about halfway across the valley and headed for the bottom of the hill, they turned and followed.

Back on Main Street the sheriff and some eager citizens raced for horses.

"Come on, boys," the sheriff shouted. "We'll catch them on that grade."

Henry, Frank, and Kid Wilson were about to catch up with the others at the bottom of the hill as the posse was beginning its ride out of town. Henry saw it coming. He looked around quickly and saw off to his left a high bluff.

"Keep going, boys," he shouted. "Hey, Kid. Come with me."

He pulled his horse hard around to the left and headed for the bluff with Kid Wilson right behind him. The posse had to pass below the bluff to continue its way up the hill in the wake of the wagon. On the backside of the bluff, Henry and Wilson dismounted and quickly settled down with their rifles.

"Just get their horses," said Henry.

Wilson didn't like the order, but he decided that he'd better obey it. As the posse rode into easy range, Wilson and Henry began firing as rapidly as they could. Seven horses dropped, and their riders rolled and tumbled on the rocky ground. The horses that were untouched bucked and reared, and there was generally panic in the posse, with horses screaming and kicking and men yelling, cursing, and scrambling for nonexistent cover. Henry and Wilson mounted up and rode off after the rest of the gang.

17

Henry Starr and Kid Wilson were the last two members of the gang to arrive back from Bentonville at Cheney's house. The wagon was there, and a quick look around revealed that everyone was accounted for except one.

"Where's Link?" asked Henry.

"We dropped him off with some folks to look after him," said Watt. "He's shot up awful bad."

Henry thought about Link and the number of bullets that must have been in his body. He could still see in his mind the image of the one eye shot out. A part of Henry felt bad for Link. Another part told him to reject the thought. Henry had never been close to Link, had never really felt anything for him. Link, like all the rest—all the rest except, perhaps, Kid Wilson—was a convenience. Link and the others were also part of the wave of unwelcome invaders who were changing the face of the Cherokee Nation. Henry could easily imagine a time in the not too distant future when his homeland would no longer be recognizable to him. He thought all of this in an instant, and he rejected any thoughts of concern for Link. The pause in the conversation was only a few seconds.

"Okay," said Henry, his mind back on business, "let's see what we got."

All the loot sacks were produced and their contents emptied onto the table. A quick but careful count was made.

"Eleven thousand five hundred," Henry announced.

"Well, boys, it's a fair haul. We'll split it up, and then we're going to have to split up this team."

"What for?" asked Frank Cheney.

"Hell," said Watt, "we just got started."

"I know," said Henry, "but we don't want to push our luck. There will be deputies all over this country looking for us, and it's only a matter of time before they get us. The Dalton boys have been wiped out up at Coffeyville, Kansas, and Cherokee Bill is sitting in jail over at Fort Smith waiting to hang. They don't have anyone left to chase but us, and they want us pretty badly. We'll each have better chances if we split up."

Watt and Cheney seemed still inclined to argue, until Kid Wilson's quiet but somehow commanding voice broke into the conversation.

"Henry's right," said Wilson. "We'd better split up."

Henry Starr had only thought that the countryside had been crawling with deputies when they had gotten after him for the twelve-hundred-dollar reward. The Starr Gang did split up and ride off in different directions, but the deputies were on all of their trails. Henry, Frank, and Kid Wilson rode off together. Watt rode alone, as did Happy Jack. Bud Tyler, having grown used to his role of teamster, kept the wagon and drove away in it to vanish in the vast numbers of white squatters and renters who were swelling the population of the Cherokee Nation. In almost no time Henry and his companions ran into a posse of sixteen, but managed to elude it after some hard riding. The unfortunate Link Cumplin somehow survived his wounds and, covered with bandages, decided to light out on his own for parts unknown. Link, not at all ready for hard riding, bought a ticket and boarded a westbound train. He was not heard of again. The following events all transpired in a matter of a few days.

Happy Jack, having noticed no one on his trail for a couple of days and being saddle weary, decided to make himself a small camp and enjoy a trail meal. He found a likely spot alongside a creek bed and unsaddled his horse, allowing it to graze freely. Tossing down the saddle to serve as a pillow, he unrolled his blanket, running it out from the saddle. After splashing some creek water onto his face, he built a small fire and put on some coffee to boil. He heated up some beans and fried some bacon. All these groceries had been part of Jack's share of the sup-plies from the chuck wagon. He ate the beans and bacon and drank a second cup of coffee, then stood up there beside his fire to stretch. Four shots blasted out of the darkness, one after the other, but Jack felt only the first one as it smashed into the small of his back. The other three came rapidly enough, however, that they all found their marks before the lifeless body pitched forward to sprawl across the campfire. Two deputy marshals stepped out of the black of the night and walked up to the body. One of them gave a heavy shove with his foot and rolled the body over out of the fire, the shirtfront smoldering. The lawmen looked down at the face of their victim, then at one another.

"Happy Jack," said the one with the heavy foot.

Riding alone down a country road, which, by the way, did not lead back to the run-down farm where the aban-doned gray woman waited, not too patiently, Watt sud-denly found himself face to face with two deputies. Not a word was spoken. Watt reached for the six-shooter in his belt. It had not yet cleared the belt when both lawmen had hauled out their pistols and fired. Two .45 slugs caught Watt in the chest, flinging him backward out of the saddle. He was dead before he hit the ground.

Henry and his two companions were still being dogged by the posse of sixteen men, and the distance between them was getting less. Spotting some suitable high ground ahead, Henry led the way to it to set up an ambush. A similar plot had worked well outside of Bentonville.

"This thing has gone on long enough," he said.

The three fugitives lay on their bellies, rifles in hand, waiting for the sixteen riders to arrive at a spot below them where they would be sitting ducks at easy rifle range. The posse rode into view, but before the members arrived at the appropriate spot, they suddenly veered off in another direction. Whether they anticipated the ambush or were simply following a wrong trail, no one could tell. Henry stood up.

"They just saved their own lives," he said.

Frank labored to his feet and stood facing Henry.

"I think it was too damn close," he said. "I'm heading south."

"Well," said Henry, "good luck to you."

Frank gave a quick nod, climbed into his saddle, and rode off without another word or a glance back.

Tulsa, in 1893, was still much closer to its embryonic form of Tulsey Town, a small Creek Indian town not far from the border of the Creek and Cherokee nations, than to the city it would become, although it was already showing some signs of its future expansion. The Katy Railroad had reached Tulsa in 1882, and many local businessmen were looking forward to prosperous futures. Gooper Johnson was one of these. One afternoon, shortly after the Bentonville incident, Johnson stood behind the counter of his undertaking establishment in Tulsa counting the coins in his coffers, when the bell above his front door tinkled. He looked up to see a young Indian man walk in. Anticipating a customer, Johnson put on his best pasty smile.

"Good afternoon, sir," he said. "How may I be of assistance?"

"My name is Henry Starr."

"Oh, my soul, the outlaw," said Johnson in a gasp as his hands reached for the ceiling over his head.

"Take it easy," said Henry.

"I have very little cash here," said Johnson, lying, "but you're welcome—"

Henry cut him off in mid sentence.

"Hold on there," he said. "I'm not here to hold you up."

"Uh, you're not?"

"No, I'm not. I'm here to do business with you."

"Uh, business?"

Gooper Johnson was still not quite at ease.

"A friend of mine," said Henry, "told me that you are the most honest man of your profession in Tulsa."

"I, uh, do pride myself on my professional integrity," said Johnson, his smile returning, his chest puffing out, and his hands coming back down to the counter before him.

"Well," said Henry, pulling some cash from his pocket, "I want to pay you for a funeral."

"May I ask—whose?"

"Someday," said Henry, "you'll read in the paper that Henry Starr has been killed. When you do, give me a decent burial."

Papers were drawn, and money was paid, and Gooper Johnson felt himself to be one of the most fortunate of men just to be alive.

Two days later Mae Morrison was walking down the main street of Nowata. As she approached a corner, Henry Starr stepped out and took her by the arm. He led her around the corner and back to a side street where Kid Wilson sat on the seat of a covered wagon, waiting. Henry helped Mae into the wagon, then climbed in after her, and Kid Wilson slapped at the team with the reins. The wagon lumbered out of Nowata heading north. The trip to Emporia, Kansas, was long, slow, and wearisome in a covered wagon, but there were no deputy marshals seen along the way, and the three travelers reached their destination with no incidents of concern. At Emporia they abandoned the wagon and purchased three railway tickets to Colorado Springs, Colorado. Henry was keeping his promise to Mae.

18

Mae Morrison stretched out on the hotel bed and sighed. She had never before been in such a large and luxurious bed. The hotel room seemed to her the height of opulence, and the hotel, itself, was the largest building she had ever been inside. In fact, it was the largest building Mae had ever seen. Her first impression on walking up in front of the hotel had been that she was approaching a castle. She had heard stories of castles. Of course, she had never seen a castle, but as she lolled on the fine bed, she thought that this must be exactly what it would be like to live in one.

Mae was totally overwhelmed by Colorado Springs. She had never been in a real city before, and everything she saw in Colorado Springs was new to her experience. And it wasn't only the city and the hotel. When she had climbed into the train at Emporia, Kansas, with Henry and his cold friend, she had embarked on the greatest adventure of her young life. The train ride with its dining car, the rapidly changing countryside, the great Rocky Mountains with snow visible up high, and finally the city and all its glamour—all this had Mae's head swimming. And the best of it all was, Mae thought, that it was only just beginning. Tomorrow she would marry Henry Starr, the handsome young Indian who was also perhaps the most sought-after bandit of the day.

The combination of the long trip from Nowata to Emporia by wagon and from Emporia to Colorado Springs by train, compounded by the intense excitement of it all, had worn Mae out. They had checked into the hotel, and

Henry and Kid Wilson had suggested going out for something to eat. Mae had declined, deciding to stay in the room and rest. She also wanted to bask in the luxury alone for a while and had secretly welcomed the opportunity. Tired though she was, she couldn't sleep, and she wasn't sorry for that. It was enough to lie on the big, soft bed and rest. In a way, it would be a shame to sleep. Mae wondered what her parents were thinking. She wondered if they were frantic for her. After all, she had told them nothing. She had simply run away with Henry when he came for her. They must be worried. But thoughts of her parents were quickly followed by thoughts of home, and home was immediately compared to her present surroundings. Mae soon dismissed her worries and, in spite of everything, began to feel drowsy.

She was not quite asleep when she heard the knock at the door. Rising slowly, she moved to the door, thinking that it must be either Henry or the Kid, and she opened it. Two strange men stood in the doorway. They appeared to be identical to Mae. They were large men, dressed in three-piece suits and heavy, dark overcoats. Each had a black handlebar moustache bristling under his nose, and a derby hat on top of his head. Each was holding out for Mae's inspection an open leather wallet with a badge pinned to its inside.

Henry Starr and Kid Wilson were walking the night streets of Colorado Springs looking for a likely place to eat. Henry thought that he had spotted a place in the next block and across the street and was about to say something when a woman appeared from out of a doorway and stepped out to meet the two men. She had a highly suggestive smile on her face to match her equally suggestive dress. Her face was heavily painted. Kid Wilson stopped in his tracks, and the lady stepped up close to him. Wilson put a hand out and touched the lady's cheek. She put her hand on his and pressed it against her powdery skin.

"Suddenly I ain't hungry," said the Kid. "You go on. I'll see you later back at the hotel."

Henry slapped Kid Wilson on the back and chuckled, then headed for the place he had spotted a moment before. It was an all-night café, and he went inside. Finding an available table, Henry sat down. A waitress soon came to his table.

"Coffee?" she asked.

"Never touch it," said Henry, "but I'd like a menu."

"Sure thing," said the waitress, turning to amble off somewhere.

Henry looked around at the people in the café, taking note of the difference in their appearance from that of the folks back home. He noticed four men in business suits come in through the front door, stop and converse briefly, then walk on in past him, presumably for a table somewhere beyond. In another minute two uniformed policemen came in. Henry felt just a bit nervous at the sight of the cops, and he tried to keep his eye on them while attempting not to seem concerned. Suddenly he felt his arms seized from behind. He struggled to his feet and tried to pull himself loose, but the grasp from behind was firm. Henry looked over his shoulder and saw that it was two of the four men he had seen enter who now held him fast. The other two stepped around in front of him and showed him badges, and the uniformed policemen were also moving toward him. He stopped struggling, and one of the men produced a pair of handcuffs.

"Who do you think you've got?" said Henry.

"Henry Starr," said the man with the manacles.

Henry shrugged.

"Well," he said, "you're right. What can I say? Let's go."

While Henry Starr was being led from the all-night café in handcuffs by four plainclothesmen and two uniformed policemen, four other policemen quietly stood in the hallway of a sleazy hotel less than a block away and drew their service revolvers out from under their long coats. At a nod, one of them threw himself against a flimsy door, and the four of them were inside in a flash. There was nothing in the dingy room but a bed. In the bed a naked woman screamed and pulled a dirty sheet up in a vain attempt to cover herself. Beside her, also naked, Kid Wilson looked up and knew that the spree was over.

"Don't shoot," he said. "You can damn well see I ain't armed."

19

Henry Starr took his second train ride. This time he rode in handcuffs, accompanied by a deputy United States marshal, and he rode from Colorado Springs, Colorado, to Fort Smith, Arkansas—back to the Fort Smith jail where Cherokee Bill sat awaiting execution, back to the jurisdiction of Isaac C. Parker, sometimes known as "the Hanging Judge." On the long ride back, Henry thought about the jail at Fort Smith. This would be his third stay there, and he knew what to expect. He also knew that this time, as the last, he had it coming. He thought about the trial. This time, he figured, there would be no bail. And he thought about the reputation of the judge. It was rumored that Judge Parker longed to be remembered as the judge who had sentenced one hundred men to hang, and it was well known that he was well on his way to that number. Henry was not just charged with robbery. He was charged with murder. He, himself, did not consider that he had committed a murder. A man had shot at him on a public road with no warning, without identifying himself, and Henry had defended himself. That was no murder. No one had been killed in the course of any of his robberies. He had been careful of that.

Henry also thought of Kid Wilson, arrested separately. He wondered what would become of the Kid and whether their paths would ever cross again. It was strange, he thought, that he cared so much about the Kid. He thought of himself as a man without friends, as a bandit leader with a gang of men gathered around him for his own convenience, but somehow this young white man had gotten to him. He liked Kid Wilson. He hoped that the Kid would get off easily. And he thought of Mae.

Mae, he decided, would be better off if she never saw him again. Whatever else happened, he told himself, he would not go around the Morrisons again. He would not try to see her. His life had been laid out for him, and it was the life of a lone outlaw. He must learn to adjust to it, to accept his fate.

At the Fort Smith depot a large crowd gathered, anticipating a glimpse of the notorious Henry Starr. Many robbers and killers were brought into Fort Smith on a regular basis, but few were genuine celebrities like Henry. The crowd included reporters and photographers, and it also included some lawmen. As the train pulled in, the excitement in the crowd mounted. A few passengers disembarked and shoved their way through the throng. Then Henry and his escort came down the stairs. The mob surged around them. Though the crowd noise was high, Henry could make out a few of the questions that were being hurled at him.

"Henry Starr," shouted a young reporter, "how did you get started on your life of crime?"

"Who was the young lady with you in Colorado?" shouted another.

Henry started to answer the second, but the questions were coming too fast.

"Who have you employed as counsel?"

Henry held up his manacled hands in a call for silence, and though he did not get silence, the questions shouted from the reporters did stop coming at him so fast. The newsmen whipped out their notepads and pencils and waited anxiously for some word from the infamous robber.

"Hey, fellows," said Henry, "I just got here."

Henry's keeper took him by the arm and tried to move forward through the crowd.

"Look out now," he said in his gruffest voice. "Let us through here."

A man stepped out of the crowd and blocked the path of Henry and the deputy. He was holding open his coat to reveal a badge.

"Deputy," he said, "let me talk to Starr. I ain't no reporter. I'm the sheriff of Benton County, Arkansas, where he robbed a bank."

Before the deputy could answer, Henry spoke up loudly.

"A man of my reputation and dignity," he said, "cannot afford to be seen holding a conversation with the sheriff of a backwoods county in Arkansas."

Then he turned to the deputy who had him in tow.

"Let's be on our way, Deputy," he said.

The crowd roared with laughter, and the reporters scrawled on their pads as quickly as they could. Henry was hustled on through the mob by the deputy and soon found himself renewing his acquaintance with the interior of the Fort Smith jail. It was as he remembered it— filthy and rank smelling. It was, as before, crowded. But this time Henry was known, and he was treated with respect by the other inmates. This time, too, he knew that he could take it.

Finding a lawyer was no problem. Several of them came around looking for work, even the redhead who had cheated Henry out of his horse and saddle earlier. Henry ran him off in record time and settled on Colonel William Cravens, a man known to be an almost constant thorn in the side of Judge Parker.

"It's not going to be easy, Henry," Cravens told him. "The man you killed was a well-liked man in Fort Smith, and he's left a widow here."

"He tried to kill me," said Henry.

"That's not going to matter much in the courtroom, I'm afraid," said Cravens. "He was a former deputy marshal, and at the time you shot him, he was working for the railroad as a detective. You were wanted for robbing the railroad. They're going to make out that he was killed in the line of duty."

"What do I care if he carried a tin badge?" said Henry. "He started shooting at me without a word of warning. He didn't identify himself. I didn't even know who he was, and I shot back. I just happen to be a better shot than he was."

"Well," said Cravens, "I want you to know that I'll do everything I can for you, but knowing Isaac Parker and his court, I don't want to give you any false hopes."

Cravens did, indeed, know the court and the judge. The trial went as the lawyer expected it would. He fought hard, but Parker controlled the courtroom proceedings and, apparently, the jury. Cravens had told Henry that Parker used a panel of handpicked "professional" jurors. The verdict was guilty. Isaac Parker looked sternly at Henry Starr.

"Henry Starr," he said, "you have been judged guilty in the first degree of the crime of murder. The cold-blooded taking away of the life of another human being is a terrible thing—an act which can only be accomplished by an inhuman monster."

Henry had heard of the delight Parker took in his moralistic tirades against the guilty, and he decided that he didn't have to listen to this one. After all, they could only hang him once. He interrupted the judge in a strong and clear voice that betrayed no emotion other than annoyance with Parker's tediousness.

"Don't try to stare me down, Old Nero," he said. "I've looked many a better man than you in the eye. Cut the rot and save your wind for your next victim."

Parker's brows drew together in a hard knot, and his face turned a deep red.

"If I am a monster," Henry continued, "you are a fiend, for I have put only one man to death, while almost as many men have been slaughtered by your jawbone as Samson slew with the jawbone of that other famous ass."

Henry was proud of the appropriateness of his literary allusions, and they were also obviously much enjoyed by the crowd, most of whom, after all, came to the trials for entertainment. Judge Parker furiously banged his gavel down and called for order. In all his days on the bench no prisoner had ever spoken to him like that. What was worse, he knew that he could do no more to Henry than what he had already planned to do. His next line was rote. He had used it many times before, but he couldn't think of a better one, so, instead, he simply delivered it with as much fury as he could muster, leaning forward as if he would leap over his desk at Henry's throat.

"Henry Starr," he said, his voice trembling with rage, his eyes fastened with hatred on Henry, "I sentence you to hang by the neck until you are dead—dead—DEAD."

20

Having been tried and sentenced, Henry was placed in an individual cell to await his execution. Symbolically, the cell window offered a commanding view of the famous Fort Smith gallows, the gallows built to accommodate six condemned men at once, the gallows with the thirteen steps to climb, the gallows that had sent so many men to untimely deaths, some perhaps deserved, others perhaps not; the gallows by means of which, it was persistently rumored, Isaac C. Parker longed to send one hundred men to their individual eternities. In spite of his better judgment, Henry spent a good deal of his time looking out the window upon that notorious instrument of death. He was standing in this particular posture thinking the thoughts that the view naturally inspired when he heard footsteps in the hallway followed by a rattling of keys just at his back. He turned to face his cell door as it was opened by a guard.

"You have a visitor, Starr," said the guard, stepping aside to allow the entrance into the cell of the portly Colonel Cravens, then shutting and locking the door again behind the lawyer.

"Hello, Henry," said Cravens.

Henry noticed the long look on the face of the colonel.

"Hey, Colonel," he said, "it's okay. I know you did what you could. And I did kill the man."

Cravens expelled a long and deep sigh, then helped himself to a seat on the wretched cot that served as Henry's bed.

"You're not going to hang, Henry," he said. "At least, not for a while. I have taken out a writ appealing your case to the United States Supreme Court on the basis of nine procedural errors. So don't give up hope yet. I haven't."

"You mean there's a chance," said Henry, "that I won't help old Parker on the way to his goal of stretching one hundred necks on his gallows?"

"There's a chance," said the lawyer. "There's a chance."

Time passed slowly in the prison. The routine was always the same. Most of the time Henry, like the other prisoners, spent alone in his small cell, either lying in his cot or staring out the window. At regular, though not frequent, intervals, the convicts were let out of the cells and marched single file by prison guards outside to an exercise yard where they were allowed to mill around more or less freely, although under very close scrutiny, for a brief period of time, before being marched back into their cells the same way they had been brought out. On one such occasion Henry had just stepped back inside his cell and was waiting for the guard to latch the door behind him when a shot rang out somewhere out in the hallway. Henry turned on instinct, and the guard had vanished. The door remained unlocked. Chaos erupted in the corridor.

At the far end of the hallway eighteen-year-old Crawford Goldsby, known as Cherokee Bill, also awaiting execution, had stepped obediently into his cell and somehow produced a six-shooter from somewhere. Before the guard behind him had a chance to react, before any of the guards in the corridor had closed the doors behind any of the prisoners, Cherokee Bill had spun and fired, killing the guard, Larry Keating, instantly. Keating had dropped in his tracks. Guards and prisoners alike were looking, trying to see what had happened, as Cherokee Bill thrust his head and right arm out of the cell and fired a second shot down the crowded corridor. A few guards had figured out where the shot had come from and were running toward the far end of the hall, but when Cherokee Bill had fired the second shot, they scurried quickly around and retreated. The prisoners had all sought the safety of their cells.

Soon the guards had clustered up at the opposite end of the hallway from Cherokee Bill, and the remaining prisoners, including Henry Starr, were caught between the guns of the young condemned outlaw on one hand and the guards on the other. Guards fired a few random shots down the hallway. There was really nothing for them to fire at, as Bill had ducked back inside his cell. From inside his cell, which was practically at the end of the row near where the guards were huddled, Henry could make out the voices of the guards between gunshots.

"Who the hell is it, anyway?" he heard one guard ask.

"That's Larry that's down," said another.

"Larry, is it?" answered the first voice. "Then I think . . ."

As he spoke, the guard slowly peeked around the corner to get a look down the hallway, and as he did, Cherokee Bill sent another pistol shot in that general direction. The guard didn't finish his sentence, as he quickly jerked himself back behind cover.

"Yeah," he said. "That's Cherokee Bill."

"Where the hell did he get that gun?" said another guard.

"How do I know?" said the first. "We found one in his cell just the other day and took it away from him." Then he turned to yet another guard, one who had thus far kept quiet. "Go get some shotguns," he ordered.

The quiet guard, glad for the opportunity to leave the

immediate vicinity, raced away in obedience. He was soon back, however, and each guard had a shotgun.

"Let him have it," someone shouted, and shotgun blasts resounded down the corridor and into the cells. Henry thought that it sounded like a small war. Pellets ricocheted up and down the hall and into the cells, and the already stuffy atmosphere was filled with thick smoke and the smell of burnt powder. The shooting stopped when the guards had all fired their initial blasts, and there was a moment of silence while they were busy reloading. Cherokee Bill jumped out into the hall and fired three pistol shots into that silence, then jumped back into the safety of the cell. Then there was a second roar of shotguns. Henry huddled far into the corner of his cell until the calm of the next reloading period. Then he eased himself close to the cell door.

"Guards," he called out. "Guards. It's Henry Starr."

"Keep back out of the way, Starr," came the answer.

"Listen to me," said Henry. "Hold your fire a minute. Let me go talk to him."

"Are you crazy?"

"Didn't you say that was Cherokee Bill?"

"Yeah, it's him all right."

"Well," said Henry, "let me go talk to him before you all kill everyone in here."

The guards were quiet for a moment. They looked at one another with questioning expressions on their tense faces. Finally one spoke.

"Hell," he said in a low voice to his comrades, "it can't hurt anything." Then, in a louder voice, shouted out to Henry, he added, "All right, go ahead."

Henry took a deep breath and scootched out into the hallway. He stood still for a moment, his heart pounding so that he imagined it could be heard by the guards and Bill and everyone in between. No shots were fired. He began to walk down the long corridor toward the cell that was the latest home of Cherokee Bill. Suddenly Bill leaned out into the hallway, gun in hand. Henry stopped still. His heart stopped pounding. It just stopped.

"Bill," he said. "Don't. It's Henry Starr."

"What are you doing here, Henry?" said Cherokee Bill.

Henry resumed his movement toward Cherokee Bill and quickened his pace.

"I came to talk you out of this," he said.

"Shit," said Cherokee Bill, as Henry stepped inside the cell to join him.

The two Cherokee outlaws sat down on the floor of the cell, Bill where he could look out into the corridor.

"What do you think you're doing, anyway?" asked Henry. "You can't get out of here."

"Well," said Bill in a sullen voice, "I can take a few of them with me."

"How many? How many shells have you got for that thing?"

Bill didn't answer. His eyes avoided those of Henry Starr.

"Bill," said Henry, "your mother wouldn't want you to do this."

At the other end of the hallway, the guards nervously awaited some sign of what might be happening in the cell of Cherokee Bill. They held their shotguns ready in anticipation of whatever might befall them. They looked anxiously at one another and down the hallway.

"What the hell are they doing down there?" said one, not really expecting an answer.

"Let's blast them both the hell out," said another.

Just then they saw at the far end Henry Starr step out into the center of the corridor. He was holding both hands high above his head, and in his left he held by its barrel a pistol.

"I'm coming out," he called.

"Well, I'll be damned," said a guard.

From that day, Henry was not only popular with the other prisoners, he was almost a hero to the guards, and he was treated very well—as well as one locked in a small, filthy, bug-infested cell can be treated. But Henry had not taken the gun from Cherokee Bill in order to ingratiate himself to the guards. When he thought about it, he wondered, himself, why he had done it. To save lives? The lives of the guards or of the other prisoners? Perhaps, though he didn't really think so. To save his own life? The chances of his being hit by a ricochet while he kept well back in his cell had been remote. Perhaps he held out some hope for Cherokee Bill as for himself that the sentence of hanging would not really take place—that there would be some kind of reprieve. If Bill had kept up his gunfight, he would surely have been killed, and then there would be no hope—not for Bill. So Henry had gone to the cell of Cherokee Bill to save Bill's life? No. That was not likely either. Since having been sentenced to hang, Bill had killed Larry Keating with no warning and for no apparent reason. And unlike Henry, Bill had killed often and unnecessarily in the course of his robberies. No. Henry Starr could not for the life of him figure out why he had done what he had done to become a hero to the guards at the Fort Smith jail.

21

Two guards walked grimly past the cell of Henry Starr and down the long corridor to stop on almost the precise spot where Larry Keating had fallen dead. One produced a ring of keys and unlocked the door to the cell of Cherokee Bill. They stepped inside and bound Bill's arms behind him; then, one on either side of the condemned man, they walked him back down the length of hallway. Inside his cell, Henry Starr, in the company of his attorney, saw them pass. Cravens, who had been talking, saw the spectacle that momentarily absorbed Henry's attention, and observed a brief but respectable period of silence until the guards and their charge had passed on through the doorway at the end of the hallway, and he had heard the heavy door clank shut behind them. Only then did he resume speaking.

"Henry," he said, "under the circumstances, I think I have to say that we won the case."

Henry stood staring vacantly out the cell window.

"I got fifteen years," he said.

"Yes," admitted Cravens, "but you won't hang."

Outside in the courtyard before the great gallows, a vast crowd had gathered. They surged and pushed against one another. Even from the distance of his cell window, Henry could see their mouths watering and their eyes bulging in anticipation of the event they were about to witness—or at least, he imagined that he could. On the other side of the tall fence that surrounded the courtyard, the unfortunate ones who could not gain entrance to the courtyard had clambered up onto the roof of a small shed so that they might see over the fence. The crowd noise suddenly increased in volume, and Henry knew that the guards had stepped out into the courtyard with Cherokee Bill. As Bill and his escorts came into Henry's view and so approached the thirteen steps leading up to the fateful platform, the crowd grew quiet. It was then that Henry noticed a dark-skinned woman in front of the crowd just before the gallows. She was weeping. As Cherokee Bill approached the bottom of the stairway, the woman stepped forward, as if she would go to him. Bill paused as he drew abreast of her, and his voice was remarkably clear to Henry up in his cell.

"Mother," Bill said, "you hadn't oughta be here."

Then he climbed the steps.

"That trick you pulled with Cherokee Bill certainly didn't hurt our case either," said Cravens.

Henry didn't seem to hear the colonel. He continued to stare down onto the scene below. The hangman had adjusted the noose around Bill's neck and was standing ready with the black hood. A deputy marshal was speaking.

"Do you have any last words?"

The crowd was absolutely silent, anticipating the final speech of the dying man. It was one of the major attractions of a public execution. Cherokee Bill knew that. He knew that he was the star attraction of this show and that his audience eagerly awaited his soliloquy. *Well,* he thought, a wry smile forming on his heavy lips, *they going to be disappointed in me again.*

"Hell," he said in a booming voice, "I came here to die, not to make a speech."

The hood was adjusted, the hangman's knot checked, Cherokee Bill was moved onto the trap, and the trap was sprung. Henry jerked as Cherokee Bill plunged into darkness. He took a deep breath, then, responding to the last thing he recalled from Cravens' conversation, he said, "No, Colonel, at least I won't hang."

Cravens left shortly after that, and Henry was alone with his feelings regarding the spectacle he had just witnessed. They were mixed feelings and strange.

22

Mary Scott Starr Walker was only one-quarter Cherokee by blood, and she did not particularly, as they say, show her Indian. Her first husband, George, known as Hop, had shown his, and of their children, Henry showed his more than the rest. In fact, Henry could easily pass for a full-blood, although he was actually only three-eighths Cherokee by blood. So the people in Washington, D.C., did not notice Mary Walker as being Indian. In fact, Mary thought, they acted pretty much as if they did not notice her at all—as if she were not even there.

Washington was intimidating, almost overwhelming to Mary. There were too many buildings, and the buildings were too big. The traffic was absolutely frightening and even menacing. Mary had a paranoid sensation that people were trying to run into her and over her, though she realized that the feeling was paranoid. (Of course, she did not know that word. In fact she did not put any word to the sensation she felt and analyzed.) She was not a voracious reader like her son, Henry. She was not much of a reader at all, and she had never understood his passion for books and for words. She vaguely wondered if that passion was not what was really at the bottom of all this—if the books were not responsible for Henry's wildness—if the excessive reading was not the reason she was wandering the strange and hostile streets of Washington, D.C. And the people seemed to be rushing everywhere. Anyone not rushing, and Mary seemed to be the only one who fit that category, was in grave danger of being run down and trampled and of not even being noticed in the process. Mary told herself that once she had accomplished her task, nothing would ever drag her back to this city, yet, until she had accomplished her task, nothing could drag her away from it.

She had been in the capital city of the United States of America for an entire month, and her money was running out. She stayed in a cheap, run-down hotel, and she ate only enough to keep her going, yet her funds were nearly depleted. She had written a letter to C. N. Walker asking him to forward her some more money, even though she knew that C.N. was far from sympathetic to her cause. Still, C.N. was her husband, and he would probably send her the money. Even if he did not, Mary had resolved that she would stay. If she had to, she would find work in order to pay her keep. She had determination. She had a cause. Even though he had left home because of her second marriage and even though she knew that he would never come back to her, she had a son, and he was in trouble. He had been in worse trouble, but it was still bad.

Mary had gone to Fort Smith and had consulted with Colonel Cravens. He had done all that he could. She was convinced of that. She liked him and she trusted him. She was grateful to the colonel, for he had saved her son from the gallows, but there was more work to be done yet. The colonel had told her that he had reached the end of his abilities. He had appealed the case to the highest court. There was no more recourse, nothing more to be done. Nothing else could be done, he had said, except . . .

"Except what?" Mary had demanded.

Colonel Cravens had felt a bit foolish. He had almost wished that he had just kept his mouth shut, but it was too late for that. He had given her that slight hope, and he had to follow it up.

"Except an appeal direct to the President of the United States for a pardon," he had said.

So Mary had scraped together all the money that she

could get her hands on, and she had gone to Washington to see the President, but she had discovered that getting to see the President was not an easy task to accomplish. On her way to Washington she had worried about what she would say to the President, she had worried about how the President would react to her tale of woe, she had worried about what kind of man the President would turn out to be. He was known to be a tough one. "Speak softly and carry a big stick," he said. She worried that the President would have no sympathy for a mother's tears, but it did not occur to her to worry about whether or not she would even be allowed to see him.

So Mary found herself in the same office day after day, facing the same expressionless face behind the same desk. She did not know the man's name, nor did she know his title. She only knew that the office in which he sat was the closest she had been able to get to the President's office and that, in order to see the President, she had to somehow get past this man. He seemed immovable.

"Mrs. Walker," he said, his voice irritable, "President Roosevelt is a very busy man. He has many more important things to see about than your problem."

"It's about my son," said Mary. "It's important to me."

"The President cannot afford to take time to visit with every mother in the country who is worried about her son."

"Not every mother in the country who is worried about her son has traveled clear to Washington from the Cherokee Nation and stayed a month to see the President," said Mary.

"Did you say 'the Cherokee Nation'?" said the bureaucrat.

Just then another man stepped into the office. Mary had not seen him before, but she could tell by his dress and his bearing that he, also, was someone of some official stature here in the capital. Whatever his business was, he seemed to put it aside for a moment to eavesdrop on what Mary was talking about. He stepped back out of the way and waited for Mary's answer to the other man's question.

"Yes," she said. "I came here all the way from the Cherokee Nation to see the President. It's the only hope my son has."

"Mrs. Walker," said the man behind the desk, his voice a bit triumphant, "are you an American citizen?"

"I'm a citizen of the Cherokee Nation," answered Mary.

"Do you mean to tell me that you've been in here pestering me half to distraction every day for well-nigh onto a month to try to get in to see the President to get a pardon for your son, and you're not even a citizen? You're not even a voter? Mrs. Walker—"

Here the eavesdropper injected himself into the conversation.

"Mrs. Walker," he said, "what did young Mr. Walker do to get himself put in prison?"

"Oh," said Mary, turning to the new speaker, "excuse me, sir. My son is not named Walker. Mr. Walker is my second husband. My first husband left me a widow with three children. My son's name is Henry Starr."

"Henry Starr. Henry Starr," repeated the newcomer. "The name sounds familiar to me. Wait a minute. That's right. Is that the young man who disarmed a fellow inmate down at the federal facility in Fort Smith, Arkansas, some time back?"

"Yes," said Mary. "Henry took the gun away from Cherokee Bill before he could kill any more guards."

"Mrs. Walker, come with me, please. I have an idea that Mr. Roosevelt will be happy to see you."

As Mary followed the man out of the office, the other tossed his unruly blond curls off of his forehead with a haughty jerk of the head and sat back down to his paperwork.

23

It was January 1903. Henry Starr, twenty-nine years old, had been in prison for nine years. After all of the appeals had been exhausted and the issue had finally been settled, Henry had been sent to the federal prison at Columbus, Ohio. He had used his time in prison to his advantage. He spent much time in the prison library, and he secured a job in the prison bakeshop. He was a model prisoner and was well-liked by guards and the warden, as well as other inmates. All in all, he took his prison time well, but it had been a crucial nine years. Henry was no longer a kid. He even had a touch of gray hair. And the world had changed around him. While Henry was still at the Fort Smith jail, Judge Parker had been deposed by his political enemies. For that, Henry had rejoiced. Parker had not lived long after his loss of power, and Henry had been sent to Columbus by the Hanging Judge's replacement, Judge Rogers.

It was 1903. The Cherokee Nation had a new Principal Chief, Samuel Houston Mayes, and the Cherokee courts had been abolished by an act of the United States Congress. The Cherokee voters, most of whom were of mixed blood and known as progressive, as opposed to traditional and mostly full-blood, had voted in favor of the allotment of tribally owned lands to private individuals. It would be the major step in the dissolution of the Cherokee Nation. In Europe, Bismarck, Oscar Wilde, Lewis Carroll, and Queen Victoria had died. In the United States Stephen Crane had passed away. The Boxer Rebellion came to an end, and the Boer War began and ended. Joseph Conrad published *Lord Jim*. Gorky's *The Lower Depths* and Strindberg's *A Dream Play* were produced, and the United States Supreme Court ruled that it was perfectly all right for the Congress to ignore Indian treaties if it is in the best interest of both the United States and the Indians to do so. Of course, Indians would not be consulted in the process of determining whether or not such an action would be in their best interests.

Henry Starr had lost nine years of his life, and the world had gone on without him. He was twenty-nine years old. It was January 1903, and Henry had been summoned to the warden's office.

A prison guard accompanied Henry to the office, opened the door, and motioned Henry to go on in. The warden sat at his desk, studying a piece of paper in his hand. He looked up as Henry stepped in.

"Henry," said the warden, "you've been a model prisoner the years you've been here. I almost hate to see you go."

"Am I being transferred, sir?" said Henry.

"I've got a letter here," said the warden, leaning back in his chair, "saying that you're to go free. It's a full pardon based largely on your bravery in securing Cherokee Bill's gun during that incident at Fort Smith. And it's signed, 'Theodore Roosevelt, President of the United States.' "

Henry was incredulous.

"The President?" he said.

"Congratulations, Henry. You've got a lot of years ahead of you yet. Make something useful out of them. You've got what it takes."

So at twenty-nine, Henry Starr walked out of prison a man nine years behind the rest of the world, yet a free man, a man with a second chance, a man full of hopes and dreams, and a man absolutely alone.

24

Kid Wilson walked down a Tulsa street, not aimlessly, nor yet in a hurry. He walked with a purpose, looking for something. Tulsa was beginning to take on some of the characteristics of the city it would become. It was 1907, and Kid Wilson had become an anachronism: an Old West outlaw in the new twentieth century, a man with no other name than "Kid," who was crowding thirty. He was also a man very much alone. No one who knew him ever knew where he had come from. His background he kept absolutely to himself. Wilson was likely not even his real name, although no one knew even that for a fact. He had cut himself off from family, and he ran alone. He ran alone, that is, except for the time he had spent as a member of the notorious Henry Starr Gang, and he had never gotten close to anyone other than Henry Starr. It was funny, he thought, that he should care so much about that Indian.

It was Henry Starr who had brought Kid Wilson on his search to Tulsa, for he had heard a rumor that Starr was out of prison and working there. Kid Wilson stopped walking and read the sign on the front of the real estate office he had come up to. He pulled a small, crumpled piece of paper out of his pocket and read a note on it, then wadded the paper and tossed it aside. He had found the right place. He opened the door and stepped inside. A man got up from behind a desk and approached him with a professional smile.

"May I help you, sir?" he said.

Kid Wilson looked the office over. Through a room to a back office he could see the backs of a man and woman and, facing them from behind a desk, sure enough, he said to himself, Henry Starr. Henry was hunkered over the desk, writing. The Kid grinned and, for an answer to the man who had greeted him, just pointed in Henry's direction.

"I'll wait," he said.

"That's fine," said the other, and he went back behind his desk to fuss with papers.

Kid Wilson figured that this man with the main desk must be Henry's boss. He chuckled to himself. It was amusing to think of any man trying to boss Henry Starr. It was equally, if not more, amusing to think of Henry Starr selling real estate. Henry looked up from his work, and his voice carried easily out to where Kid Wilson waited.

"I hope you enjoy the house," he said.

"I'm sure we will," came the voice of a young man.

"Oh, yes," added a young woman's voice.

"Well," said Henry, standing up behind the desk, "here are your keys. If there's anything more I can do for you, just let me know. And thank you very much."

"Thank you," said the young woman.

"Good-bye now," said the man.

The young couple, leaning on each other and smiling, walked out of the office and past Wilson, who stepped into the doorway to Henry's cubicle and leaned casually on the door frame.

"Somebody told me that all real estate salesmen are crooks," he said, "but this is ridiculous."

Henry looked up and saw Kid Wilson there in the doorway. Something inside made him want to jump up, run, and clap his old comrade on the shoulders, but instead he leaned back in his chair and smiled.

"Well," he said, "I've certainly got the background for it."

Then, laughing, he stood up and moved around the desk. He held out his right hand to Wilson.

"What are you doing, Kid?" he said.

"Oh, I heard you were around, and I thought I'd look you up."

"It's been a long time," said Henry. "About fourteen years, I guess."

"Yeah."

"Well, sit down, Kid. Let me get you a cup of coffee."

Wilson sat down in one of the two chairs recently vacated by the young couple while Henry went out to the coffeepot in the main office. He came back soon with one cup and set it on the desk in front of Wilson.

"You still not a coffee drinker, I see," said Wilson.

"I've never tasted it," said Henry.

"I hear you're a family man now."

"I've got a wonderful wife and a fine young son," said Henry, the pride obvious in his voice.

"Henry, Jr.?" said Wilson.

"No," said Henry. "Theodore Roosevelt Starr."

Kid Wilson leaned back and laughed.

"I heard you got a full pardon from the President, himself," he said. "So how's Mae?"

"Mae?" said Henry. "Oh. No, I don't know. No, she couldn't wait. Well, actually I never saw her again after Colorado Springs. No, I married a Cherokee girl named Olive Griffin."

"Oh, well, hell," said Kid Wilson, "they come and go. Well, Henry, real estate. Damn, that's the worst thieving you ever done yet. Do you like it? I mean, this life."

"Yeah," said Henry. "Yeah. It's fine. Just fine."

But something about Henry's voice left Kid Wilson less than convinced that Henry Starr was finding the good life totally satisfactory. He decided to change the subject.

"Well, boy," he said, "what do you think about this state of Oklahoma business?"

Henry's brows furrowed into a scowl.

"It sure wouldn't do to put in print what I think about it," he said. "This is Indian country. We're sitting right now in the Creek Nation, in this Tulsey Town, and just a few miles over yonder is the Cherokee Nation—my country."

Henry hesitated and expelled a long and weary sigh.

"But that's all in the past now," he continued. "It looks as if we're going to be the next state no matter what anyone thinks about it—especially the Indians."

"Yeah," said Kid Wilson, because he could think of nothing else to say. He was almost sorry that he had brought up the subject.

"Listen," said Henry. "You've got to come over to the house and meet my family. How about tonight? We've got lots to talk about, you and me."

"That sounds fine, Henry," said the Kid. "Thanks. Tonight will be just fine. I'm not doing a damn thing."

25

It was 1907. Henry Starr took his wife and child to Guthrie, the capital city of the new state of Oklahoma, for the grand celebration. Kid Wilson accompanied them. There were banners everywhere for "Oklahoma" and "the 46th state." There was an atmosphere of celebration and festivity seemingly permeating the very air. There was no place to escape the teeming crowds. Indians of fifty-seven different tribes and blacks and whites and some of indeterminable racial mixture rubbed shoulders with each other, crowded against each other. The formalities of the statehood ceremony were planned for and carried out outdoors because of the tremendous number of people in attendance. For the main ceremony a large platform had been constructed in the open, and the people mobbed around it. The platform was crowded with dignitaries. C. N. Haskell, the newly elected first governor of the state of Oklahoma, was up there, and Robert L. Owen, prominent Cherokee politician, now United States senator from Oklahoma, was also there. A band had been playing, followed by speeches from Haskell, Owen, and others. Finally a symbolic wedding ceremony was held in which a white man, young and handsome and dressed in white cowboy clothes, representing the Oklahoma Territory, was married to an Indian girl, beautiful in her white buckskin dress, representing the Indian Territory.

A master of ceremonies stepped forward and bellowed to the crowd through a megaphone.

"And that's the marriage of Oklahoma Territory and

Indian Territory—the union that has resulted in the creation of the forty-sixth state in the United States of America—the great state of Oklahoma."

The roar that went up from the crowd was deafening. Fireworks were set off in the background, and a few slightly rowdy celebrants fired off six-guns. In the crowd, standing beside his wife and holding his infant son, Henry Starr spoke out loud, though his voice was obscured by all the noise.

"Why is it an Indian woman and white man?" he said. "Why not the other way around?"

At that instant Kid Wilson came pushing his way through the crowd. Squeezing up to Henry, he leaned over as if to whisper in Henry's ear. Yet he did not whisper. He shouted.

"Henry," he said, "come out of this crowd."

Henry handed little Theodore Roosevelt to his mother and fought his way with Kid Wilson out of the crowd. It took some doing, but they finally got away from people to a spot where they could talk unlistened to by others.

"What's this all about?" Henry asked.

"The word's out," said Wilson, "that just as soon as Oklahoma statehood is official, Arkansas is going to ask extradition on you for that Bentonville bank job."

"That was years ago," said Henry. "I've been straight for nearly five years and spent the nine previous in the pen. That's counting the Fort Smith jail time."

"I guess them hillbillies don't never give up."

"Can they do that to me, Kid?" asked Henry. "I got a pardon from the President."

"What I've been hearing is that the pardon just only covered the crime that you was in prison for at the time. You got pardoned for that, but not for anything else. Arkansas still has a live warrant on you, and it's enforceable."

"But the new governor of Oklahoma will have to agree to it. Right?"

"That's right," said Kid Wilson.

Henry paced away from Kid Wilson a few steps, then paced back. He scratched his head underneath the white Stetson he wore as a dress hat.

"Kid, you've got to help me," he said. "I'm taking my family home. You stay around the capital here and find out what they decide. Call me just as soon as you know. Do you know the number?"

"I've got it wrote down here," said Wilson.

"All right," said Henry. "I'll be waiting for your call."

Henry left Kid Wilson and headed back into the crowd to find his wife and child. Fireworks and gunshots continued. The celebration would last long into the night.

26

Henry Starr and Kid Wilson rode out of Tulsa into the night. They rode two stolen horses, and they rode west. They had no real specific plans other than to lose themselves somewhere. Henry had gotten the telephone message from Guthrie, and the message had been that Governor Haskell had approved the Arkansas request for extradition. Kid Wilson had stolen the two horses and met Henry back in Tulsa to join him on the getaway. Henry would not voluntarily go back to prison. He had never had much respect for Arkansas or its general population, and this incident simply strengthened his impression. He had not been able to face his wife with the news that he would once more become a fugitive from justice, would once again "go on the scout," so he had secretly made his arrangements with Kid Wilson, left Olive Starr a note of brief explanation and apology, and quietly slipped out of her life.

I should have known all along, he had told himself, *that it just wasn't meant to be. Ever since that first arrest, everything has worked toward making me a criminal. I've tried to go against it, and it won't work. They won't let me alone.*

Henry was sorry to leave Olive and Theodore Roosevelt, but he accepted his fate stoically. His sense of having been manipulated, if not by the fates, then certainly by the minions of the foreign legal system that had been thrust upon his people, allowed him to face this new twist with a bitter stoicism. He would not pine away over his loss. He would accept his fate and ride with it.

A man is always alone, he told himself.

Then he thought of Kid Wilson and his companionship —his friendship.

That, too, will end, he thought. *No matter how things may seem for a time, a man is always alone.*

Henry Starr and Kid Wilson rode by night. During the daylight hours they would find a place to sleep and hide until the safety of darkness returned. They slept in corn bins and barns, and they maintained this pattern until they felt that they were far enough away from Tulsa to be a bit safer. They had left the rocky foothills and wooded countryside of eastern Oklahoma behind and were riding across rolling prairie when Henry made the decision.

"I think we're far enough from home to cut out this night riding," he said.

"I could sure go for a genuine home-cooked breakfast," said Kid Wilson.

Henry looked ahead at a farmhouse that lay in their line of travel.

"Let's try that place," he suggested.

As the two riders moved into the yard, the farmer, a burly man about fifty years old, came out the front door of the house.

"Fall off, boys," he shouted, his voice open and friendly.

Henry and Wilson dismounted.

"Howdy," said Henry.

The farmer turned his head back toward the house.

"Two more for breakfast, Mother," he roared, "and hungry ones, too, if I'm a judge."

"You certainly got that one right, mister," said Henry, "and we do appreciate your kind invitation. Is it all right if we water our horses here before we go in?"

"Right over there. Water and feed. Help yourselves. We don't get many visitors out here. A bit off the beaten path, we are, I'd say."

"Well," said Kid Wilson, "we're just as glad to have found you in our path."

At the breakfast table the jolly farmer talked incessantly, although somehow that fact didn't seem to interfere any with his eating. He ate mounds of potatoes, any number of fried eggs, great stacks of pancakes, and countless slices of bacon. His wife was constantly refilling his coffee cup. Henry and Kid Wilson did their share of damage to the larder, having been for several days with only trail food, and the farmer's talk didn't bother them at all.

"Yeah, boys," the farmer said while chewing, "I've done right well. I settled this farm the day of the big opening back in '89. Three hundred and twenty acres. And to prove that hard work pays off, I just last month turned down an offer of sixteen thousand for it."

He took a great slurp from his coffee cup.

"Well, sir," said Henry, "I congratulate you on your staying power. You have a fine-looking place here."

The big opening of '89, thought Henry. *The high-handed taking away of land from Indians followed by the casual giving of it to the whites. Worse. To the poor white trash.* This farmer had probably had nothing before the opening. Otherwise there would have been no reason for him to have taken part in the process. This was his home. Then he had no other. He had nothing before. The government had taken the land away from Indians so that poor whites, with nothing, could take the land for themselves and, in a few years, have assets worth sixteen thousand dollars. Yet the farmer was hospitable, and Henry could not bring himself to hate the man. He could hate the government that had perpetrated the grand theft, but not the farmer.

Riding out from the farm later, Henry did not reveal any of these thoughts to Kid Wilson.

"Yes, sir," he said, "for genuine, unaffected, all wool and a yard wide hospitality, the Oklahoman may be equaled but not surpassed."

"Yeah," said Kid Wilson, "it was a good breakfast."

They made a camp that night. The land was barren and harsh. They ate hardtack and jerky, and over a small fire they boiled coffee for Kid Wilson. Henry drank water.

"Where you reckon we are by now?" said Wilson.

"I think we're about dead center in that No Man's Land," said Henry.

"Is that still Oklahoma?" said Wilson.

Henry chuckled.

"Just barely," he said.

Oklahoma's panhandle, formerly known as No Man's Land, is the only state area so designated that, pictured on a map, is worthy of its name. An elongated and nugatory excresence shooting off into the west from the extreme northwestern corner of the state, it's not much more than a wide border between Texas and southern Colorado and Kansas. Pictured from the back of a horse, it's desolate, barren, windswept, and lonely. No Man's Land seems the best name for it then, for it has the appearance of a land that no man would want or could survive in. Its only real function seems to be to prevent its northern neighbors from having to touch Texas.

"I figure Kansas is only about sixteen miles over there," Henry went on. "Texas is about twenty. And we can't be more than about sixty or seventy miles out of Colorado and New Mexico."

"I don't want to go back to Colorado," said Wilson.

"I don't have the fondest memories of the place, myself," said Henry. "No, I think we'll try our luck in New Mexico, maybe. But first we need to finance our trip. There's a little town just across the line in Kansas."

"Yeah?"

"It has a nice little bank."

27

Along toward sundown the next day, Henry and Kid Wilson found themselves a short distance from the Kansas line and even closer to another farm. Their last stop at a farm had been successful, Henry thought, and there was no reason to ride on into Kansas during the evening hours. The little town he had in mind was just across the border.

"Let's check out the local hospitality," he said to Kid Wilson. "If we can spend the night here, we can get an early start for the state line in the morning."

A few more minutes found them inside the farmhouse, trying their best not to appear as bored as they really were. The farmer and his wife had two rather drab daughters, and Henry and Wilson had happened in on an evening when a young man had come courting. The courted daughter was playing the piano, accompanied by her beau on the violin. The father was snugged down in an overstuffed chair, smoking his pipe and enjoying the music tremendously. The tune was "Drink to Me Only with Thine Eyes." Off in the kitchen, the mother and the other daughter were preparing the supper. Henry staunchly tried not to wince each time he heard a sour note from either the piano or the violin, while Kid Wilson, who couldn't tell a sour note from a sweet one, was simply suffering in general.

Suddenly, with no warning, the mother called out from the kitchen in a shrill voice.

"Soup's on," she said.

The music came to a squawking halt with no attempt at a formal ending, and the family all rushed to the table. Nor was the gentleman caller shy in his approach to dinner. Henry and Wilson were the last ones to reach the table and to sit. There was a hurried grace, and an even bigger hurry to clean all the platters. When Kid Wilson perceived that there was nothing left to eat, he leaned back from the table.

"That was a mighty fine meal, ladies," he said.

"And, I might add," said Henry, "exceeded only by the fine hospitality of this entire family."

"Why, thank you, boys," said the farmer. "We do pride ourselves on our Christian charity."

The farmer's wife then stood up. She wiped her hands on her dirty apron, and flour dust flew.

"Why don't we all go on back in here to the easy chairs and just enjoy some more good music," she said. "I do love to hear good music played."

Henry thought to himself that he, too, loved to hear good music played, but he doubted that he would hear any played in this house. Kid Wilson had a mild touch of panic. He didn't think that he could stand much more of the duet and their particular brand of music, but Kid Wilson was not one to accept unpleasantness calmly. He quickly formulated a plan.

"I don't know much about it, myself," he said with sudden inspiration, "but I'm sure that my friend here would like nothing better, since he's something of a musician, himself."

Henry shot Wilson a threatening glance, but before he could do anything more, the farmer's wife had picked up Wilson's cue.

"Oh, really?" she said excitedly. "What do you play?"

"Oh," said Henry, "I just fiddle around a bit."

"With what?" said the good wife.

"Why, the fiddle, of course."

Henry's little joke received a round of polite and good-natured laughter, followed by the insistence of all that he give them a sample of his musical skill. The young man rushed up to Henry and thrust the fiddle at him, so Henry gave in to the demands. He tested the unfamiliar instrument with a squawk or two, tightened a couple of strings, then charged right into a rousing rendition of "The Texas Quickstep." Soon all were stomping feet and clapping hands. The young couple began to dance. The farmer and his wife joined them, and finally even Kid Wilson and the leftover daughter began to tromp the floorboards. Henry played four or five tunes before the farmer called a halt to the festivities on the grounds that the hour was late and he would have to rise early in the morning to get at his chores.

"Boys," he said, "I wish I could do you better than send you to the barn, but we just ain't got the room in the house, what with four of us in here already."

As he spoke to Henry and Wilson, he gave a hard and meaningful stare to the young man who was courting his daughter. That swain moved to pick up his hat.

"Well," he said, "I reckon I oughta be heading on home. I guess it's getting kind of late. Good night all."

He smiled sappily at his sweetheart, who followed him out the door to bid him good night. Henry laid aside the fiddle.

"The barn will suit us just fine," he said. "Don't give it another thought."

"Well," said the farmer, "good night, then."

Henry and Wilson made their way to the barn and found themselves each a pile of hay in which to build a nest for the night. It didn't take them long to fall into a deep sleep. But a lengthy rest was not in the cards for Henry and Wilson that night. It had been only a couple of hours before each man felt a hand on his shoulder shaking him out of his slumber. They awoke gazing sleepily into the eyes of the two daughters, whose eyes were not at all sleepy.

"What—what are you doing here?" asked Henry, rubbing his eyes.

"Everyone's asleep," said the first daughter.

"So were we," said Henry.

"We just thought that you all might like to have some company out here," said the second daughter.

"Well," said Kid Wilson, and he pulled the one who was hanging over his face down to him, crushing her lips with his.

"You two had better get back inside before your folks find out where you've gone to," said Henry.

"Oh, it's all right," said the one pushing herself at Henry. "They won't wake up for a while. They're sound sleepers."

"Ain't no hurry, Henry," said Wilson.

Henry pushed the girl away from himself and pulled on his boots. He stood up.

"Get your boots on, Kid," he said. "We've got a long ride ahead of us this morning."

Kid Wilson didn't respond, and Henry gave him a kick.

"Come on, Kid," he said, the tone of his voice and the expression on his face leaving no room for argument.

The unexpected nocturnal visit resulted in Henry and Wilson's finding themselves in Kansas and on the outskirts of their destination much earlier than they had planned. The town was not yet quite awake. They settled down on the side of a gradual slope with a good view of the main street to wait for the bank to open. Kid Wilson was sullen.

28

The bank job had been easy. Almost too easy, Henry thought. As soon as they had seen the first bank employee show up and unlock the door, they had headed on down into the still sleepy town. By the time they had arrived at the bank, a few others were at work. They had hitched their horses out front and calmly walked up to the front door. Then, with a glance at each other, they had drawn their pistols and burst through the front door almost simultaneously. Henry had shouted out his famous order.

"Hands up and hands steady."

The people in the bank had been thoroughly terrified and totally cooperative, and Henry Starr and Kid Wilson had ridden away with a sackful of money. They had not ridden far from town when Kid Wilson called out to Henry.

"Hold it," he said.

"What's wrong, Kid?"

"Ain't nothing wrong, Henry," said the Kid. "I just want my share of that money right here and now."

"Kid," said Henry, "just because that bunch of bankers was such easy pickings doesn't mean that they won't send out a posse on our trail. We need to get farther away from this place before we slow down any. Come on."

"No," said the Kid. "Divide it now."

"What for?"

"Because I ain't going the same direction you are."

"What?"

"It's time we split up, Henry. I ain't riding any farther with you. You're on your own."

Henry thought, *I've always been on my own. That's just a fact of life. A man is always alone.* But when he spoke again to Kid Wilson, it was not to offer him that bit of philosophy.

"All right, Kid," he said. "We'll do it."

Henry climbed down out of the saddle, and Kid Wilson did the same. The Kid looked to Henry as if he were ready to spring into action. He had the look of a coiled rattlesnake. Henry pulled a bandanna out of his pocket and spread it on the ground, then dumped the money out of the sack onto the bandanna to count it.

"This is kind of sudden, Kid," he said. "Where will you go?"

"You spoiled my night for me last night," said Kid Wilson. "I aim to go back to that farm and get what I would have got last night if it hadn't been for your damned holiness."

"Kid," said Henry, "that farmer fed us and put us up. We owe him better than to do him dirt."

"Well, if you feel like you owe him something, you pay him. Me, I feel like I owe them two anxious gals something, and I'm going to give it to them."

Henry studied Kid Wilson's face. It was cold—determined. It was probably senseless to argue further with the Kid, but Henry didn't want to give it up just yet.

"If that old man catches you with his daughters, he'll likely kill you," he said.

"He might die trying," said Kid Wilson.

Henry stood up slowly, keeping his eyes on the Kid. Kid Wilson stepped back a couple of paces and pushed his coattail back out of the way of his six-gun.

"Kid," said Henry, "you're not going back there."

Kid Wilson reached for his gun, but he fumbled an instant too long. Henry's .45 was out first, and the blast of the shot seemed to echo over the expansive Kansas prairie. Kid Wilson was thrown backward into the dust, a gaping hole in his chest. He wasn't quite dead. Henry could hear the rasping of his breath. He wouldn't last long, though, and he didn't appear to be conscious of anything around him. He was probably in shock. Henry gathered up the money in the bandanna and stuffed it back into the bag. He had killed his second man, and this time it was a man who had been his friend, at least as close to a friend as Henry had ever had. He wondered briefly if the farmer's daughters had been worth it. Then the ragged breaths of Kid Wilson suddenly ceased. *A man is always alone,* Henry thought. He climbed on his horse and rode away.

In spite of his earlier misgivings, he found himself riding toward Colorado. He rode a good part of the morning away and had just topped a small rise when he heard the baying of hounds. He stopped his horse and surveyed the landscape all around. Off in the distance and moving in his direction, he could make out the figures of two riders with dogs on leashes. There wasn't much in the way of cover, so Henry led his horse down the far side of the rise and trailed the reins. He went back up on top on foot and crouched down low to await the riders. It seemed like a long wait, but Henry had cultivated patience over the years. The riders made the foot of the rise without spotting Henry. He stood up, gun in hand.

"What do you fellows want?" he demanded.

The riders pulled up hard.

"We're just out hunting," said one.

Henry walked down the rise toward the riders, keeping his .45 leveled at them.

"Shut those dogs up," he said.

With some difficulty the two men managed to do as they were told.

"I think you're trailing me," said Henry.

"No," said the second of the two. "No, we ain't."

"Throw your guns down there," said Henry.

The two again did as they were told.

"Now back up."

As the two men with their horses and dogs backed away from where they had dropped their guns, until he felt there was enough space between them, Henry moved forward. He holstered his .45 and picked up their guns, one at a time, and emptied the shells out of them. Then he threw the guns back down. He pulled his own gun back out and looked again at the riders.

"Say," he said to one of them, "don't I know you?"

The rider grew even more nervous. He had been a Colorado Springs policeman a few years back. Henry Starr did, indeed, know him. He had helped to arrest Henry in the Colorado Springs all-night café. He thought about lying, trying to deny that he had ever seen Henry Starr, but he knew that he would never get away with that.

"Well," he said, "you might."

"Yeah," said Henry. "It's been a while. I ought to kill you."

"You can't do that," said the man. "I don't have a gun."

Henry bent down to pick up a gun from the ground. He tossed it at the man. The man caught it, fumbled with it for a moment, then held it more or less steady.

"It ain't loaded," he said.

"You got shells in your belt," said Henry. "Load it."

"No. Wait. Please."

Henry looked at the man. He was shaking from fear. *A typical lawman*, he thought. *They act brave when they've slipped up on a man unexpected and got him covered, but face up to them and they'll crawfish every time.* Suddenly the man didn't seem worth killing. It would make as much sense to kill the dogs—maybe more.

"Hell," he said, "take your dogs and get out of here. Go on."

The two men wasted no time obeying this last order. They were soon out of sight, riding back in the direction from which they had come. And not long after that, Henry Starr crossed the border into the state of Colorado.

29

He spent a few days alone, riding and camping, existing on his trail food and on small game. It was 1908, and Henry Starr was thirty-five years old. The Cherokee Nation, though powerless, still existed on paper to allow the federal government and the new state of Oklahoma to continue the long and arduous task of legalizing land transfers. William C. Rogers was nominal Principal Chief. It was the year that Wayne Brazil assassinated the killer of Billy the Kid, former sheriff Pat Garrett, near Las Cruces, New Mexico. Henry Starr could see the world that he had known changing around him. Those days alone in Colorado, he remembered his boyhood days in the Cherokee Nation. He recalled the times when the only white people he saw were poor whites moving west or the land renters in the Cherokee Nation—the times when the Cherokees looked down on whites as members of a less fortunate race. The Cherokee Nation had been a thriving little republic, with its own school system, its own capital city, its voting districts and legal system. The Nation had, in those days, a national council elected by popular vote, and a national budget with education as the top-line-item priority. It had no national debt, but its budget had been largely supported by the rent money from white ranchers and farmers who settled among the Cherokees. The renters had been at once the mainstay and the downfall of those golden years. For when the numbers of whites in the Cherokee Nation became great, the federal government moved to protect their interests by beginning to

erode the powers of the small Nation. The end result was
Oklahoma.

Henry looked back on all this with a strange mixture of
bitterness and resignation, and when he came upon the
small town of Amity, Colorado, though he had money in
his pockets from the last bank robbery, money which, after all, he had not even had to divide with the late, unfortunate Kid Wilson and had not found any place yet to
spend, he, therefore, robbed its bank.

A posse rode out from Amity, but Henry eluded them
easily. It was another day when he spotted a windmill and
rode toward it for water. When he got closer, he saw that
there were three men there already. They were filling
water barrels. Henry rode on over to them.

"Can I water here?" he asked.

"Sure. Help yourself," answered one of the men.

Henry watered his horse, got himself a drink, and re-
filled his canteen.

"Would there be a place around here where I might
spend the night?" he said.

A big black-bearded man, carrying a shotgun, stepped
forward.

"I live about a mile north," he said. "You're welcome to
stop there for the night."

Henry helped the men load their water barrels into a
wagon. One man climbed aboard and drove the wagon
off. The other two began walking, leading their horses.
Henry followed them along. Soon they were moving beside a prairie dog town, and the man with the shotgun
spied one dog beside its hole. He raised the gun and fired.
The prairie dog scurried for its hole.

"Here," said Henry, "let me have that dog gun."

By the time they had walked the mile to the homestead,
Henry had killed eight prairie dogs and had returned the
shotgun to its owner. The two homesteaders sat down
outside their sod house to clean their prairie dogs, tossing

the skins to two skinny curs, who pounced on them hungrily. Henry chuckled.

"Now, there's nothing an Indian likes better than a genuine dog stew," he said, "but I believe that a couple of these ancient pups stood on their hind legs and barked defiance at the buffalo before the days of the Santa Fe Trail."

The black-bearded prairie dog skinner looked up from his task briefly.

"Young man," he said, "I've traveled the world over carrying the gospel to the heathen, and I've always seen fit to eat what the good Lord sends my way."

Henry smiled, but he kept to himself his thought that it had been he, not the good Lord, who had sent this batch of prairie dogs the old man's way. The stew was prepared by two women who appeared from inside the soddy, and Henry did his part in emptying the pot. He settled back for some casual conversation before time to hit the hay, but the black-bearded missionary surprised him.

"Well," he said, "we had better be started if we're to be on time for church. You'll be joining us, of course?"

The question had been directed at Henry, who immediately stood up and put on his hat.

"Of course," he said.

Church turned out to be a camp meeting under a brush arbor. Henry looked around at the dry, barren prairie and wondered where they had gotten the brush. There was a fair-sized gathering of homesteaders there. Henry found himself seated in the midst of a sweating crowd in a revival mood. An old soldier in the remnants of a Union Army uniform had been testifying for several minutes.

"And I'll just close my testimony with this here thought for all of you," he said.

Henry was relieved to hear that the testimony was about to close.

"Every last mother's son and daughter of us has sinned."

The congregation roared "amens."

"And fell short of the glory of God."

More "amens" came from the crowd, and Henry felt conspicuous.

"Amen," he said.

"But by the grace of God, we'll rise to that glory once again come Judgment."

As the old soldier sat down, he was patted on the back by all who could reach him, while more "amens" were shouted. There was applause, and a couple of nonconformists roared out, "Hallelujah!" The black-bearded missionary, Henry's host, got back up before the congregation.

"I want to thank our brother," he droned, "for that fine testimonial, and now I'd like to ask the stranger in our midst if he wants to share a few words with us tonight."

There were shouts of approval, and Henry felt hands on him from all sides, pushing and urging him to give an affirmative answer to the missionary's question. Henry somehow felt that it would be unsafe to refuse. There is little in life more dangerous than righteous wrath aroused. He rose to his feet.

"Well, my friends," he said, "I will tell you what. The sentiments of the brother preceding are my sentiments exactly. I hope that the associations of the evening remain in happy retrospect, and I believe that you ministers, here, are doing a great work in this community."

As the meeting was breaking up, and people were shaking Henry's hand and congratulating him on a fine speech, he was thinking to himself that it had been, indeed, a fine speech. He had not lied at all, for, to begin with, he agreed with the old soldier that nobody is perfect. Second, when he had hoped that the evening's associations would remain happy, he had been looking at the prettiest girl in the crowd, and, finally, he had praised the work of the preachers in the community, because, if they were to keep up their good work, he figured, they would soon rid their community of pesky prairie dogs.

He managed to survive all of the preaching and to get a good night's sleep and a good breakfast from his host. In the morning he resumed his journey, which was generally west. By evening he had gotten into the mountain country of Colorado, and he was riding down a narrow mountain pass. As he rounded a curve in the pass, he suddenly brought his horse to a halt. There before him were two mounted men with rifles. He looked over his shoulder, and two more appeared behind him. There were four rifles leveled at him. He slowly raised his hands above his head and shrugged.

"I should have listened to the Kid," he said.

"What?" said one of the horsemen.

"Oh, nothing," said Henry, then with a little disgust in his voice, added, "Colorado."

30

He was caught fair, and Henry accepted his fate with calm resignation. He was sentenced to serve from seven to twenty-five years in the Colorado State Penitentiary at Canyon City, and he began his sentence with a steadfast determination. As before, he was a model prisoner. He did what he was told to do without hesitation. He was a favorite of guards and prisoners alike. He spent some time at hard labor, working on a road gang, but soon he was made boss of the gang. When he was able, as before, he spent time in the prison library. While Henry was serving the first year of his sentence, William Howard Taft became the twenty-seventh President of the United States. At Fort Sill, Oklahoma, the famous and once feared Geronimo died, and Red Cloud, who had once forced the United States Army to abandon a fort along the Bozeman Trail, died in South Dakota. Butch Cassidy and Harry Longbaugh, known as the Sundance Kid, were rumored to have been killed by law officers in Bolivia.

As Henry spent more time in the prison, he found that his privileges increased. He had more time to spend in the library, and he read books on law and on criminology. He read newspapers as well, and he read of the death of Mark Twain in 1910 and of the 1912 Olympic Games in Stockholm, where a Sac and Fox Indian from Oklahoma named Jim Thorpe won both the decathlon and pentathlon championships. Yes, Henry thought, the world was rapidly changing around him. He vaguely wondered how many years he would spend shut away from the world this time, and how strange he would find it upon his release.

But the prison was being too kind to Henry, and he had more time on his hands than he knew what to do with. He decided to write a book in which he would tell his life story. After all these years Henry still felt he had been forced into a life of crime, and he felt an urge at this stage in his life to leave a record of his side of the story. He sat in the prison library with a stack of paper and a pencil. He had been required to obtain permission from the warden for this undertaking, but that had not been difficult.

He stared for a few moments at the blank paper there before him, scratched his head, and then began to write.

I was born near Fort Gibson, Indian Territory, on December 2, 1873, and am of Scotch-Irish-Indian ancestry. My father, George Starr, was a half-blood Cherokee Indian; my mother, Mary Scott, is one-quarter Cherokee. There were three children by their union— Elizabeth, the eldest, Addie, the second, and myself, Henry George Starr, the youngest. I might mention that I was born in a cabin, the inevitable log cabin, close to Fort Gibson, one of the oldest forts in the west. It was here Sam Houston came when he fled from his beautiful wife and the governorship of Tennessee, and later married the fair Indian maiden, Talihina. Sam Houston was also famous for his ability to put much fire-water under his belt, and his accomplishments along that line were the envy of every Indian and soldier in that region.

Washington Irving also visited Fort Gibson, and it was while ruminating along the banks of the beautiful Grand River, that he wrote "The Bee Hunt" and other stories.

The book occupied all of Henry's spare time until it was concluded, and it wasn't long after he had finished that he was called in to see the warden, it was hoped for the last time. He had received his parole, and he had been issued a civilian suit. It was 1913, and Woodrow Wilson was President of the United States. Cecil B. DeMille had produced *The Squaw Man*, and the United States Congress had passed the 16th amendment in order to allow an income tax. Henry had read about all these things, but, standing before the warden, he wondered what the world was like out there. The warden looked up at Henry from behind a cluttered desk. His expression was friendly but serious.

"Henry," he said, "do you understand the terms of this parole?"

"Yes, sir," said Henry, "I think so."

"You know," continued the warden, "the last time you were released from prison, you had been pardoned. You were free. This is different. You're not free. Not quite. You're on parole."

"Yes, sir. I realize that."

"You're going to have to find gainful employment here in Colorado, at least until you've served this out."

Henry did as he was told. At forty years of age, he found a job in a hash house in Pueblo.

The job at the hash house was all right for a while. For a while it was new, and when the newness had worn off, Henry was able to endure it longer by calling up from within himself feelings of self-righteousness. He was keeping to the straight and narrow. He was earning, not much money, but he was earning it. He was making honest wages for honest work. He was, he told himself, a reformed man. He had written to Olive to let her know where he could be found and what the terms of his parole were. Did she want to come to Pueblo and bring little Theodore Roosevelt? The money wasn't much, but they could get along on it. She had answered that she wasn't at all anxious to remove herself and her child to a strange place far away from home. She hoped that he was doing well and that his life would be better in the future. The letter, Henry thought, was just a bit cold. Well, he couldn't really blame her. He certainly hadn't done right by her in the past, and he didn't really have anything to offer at present. He thought that it would have been nice to be able to live a quiet and normal life with his wife and child. He wondered what Theodore Roosevelt looked like. He must be getting to be a big boy. Henry reminded himself that the life of a normal workingman, a husband and a father, just wasn't in the cards for him. He felt a pang of guilt for having brought Olive into his life, for having allowed himself to believe that it would work, for having convinced her that it would.

There was a waitress in the hash house, Laura, who had

displayed an interest in Henry almost from the time he had gone to work there. She was white, blond, in her mid-thirties. She was a reasonably attractive woman, though she showed the signs of a rough life in her features. Henry walked her home after work late one evening. He stayed all night with her, and he thought about Olive and his son back in Tulsa, and for the first time in nearly twenty-three years he felt really guilty.

But Olive's letter had been cold. In spite of the guilt, the nights with Laura became more and more frequent. They became regular, and as Henry grew more comfortable with Laura, he also grew less patient with the hash house and more restless. He was not a man who had been cut out for a regular life, he reminded himself. The episodes in his youth with the federal lawmen, the word about the planned Arkansas extradition from the new state of Oklahoma following his pardon (which, by the way, had been proved later to be a mistake, as the governor of Oklahoma had refused the request of Arkansas), all of these had demonstrated clearly to him over the years that he was a man marked at birth for life as a criminal and a fugitive. He was only fooling himself in Pueblo at the hash house, he thought. It couldn't last because it simply was not meant to be. Yet a part of him wanted to keep trying. He thought of his family in Tulsa and of the rewards of the simple, ordinary home life. Something deep within him longed for that life.

Then he received another letter from Tulsa.

He was sitting quietly with Laura in her small apartment after work one evening. The room was, like Henry's own, rather shabbily furnished and badly in need of repair. He was thinking how drab was his existence in Pueblo, moving back and forth from the hash house to the dingy apartments. His meager wages didn't allow for much else. He and Laura had made love—no, he thought, they had not made love. They had engaged in an urgent biological activity together. It had been satisfying, but it was a satisfaction that all animals could attain. However, they each accepted it for what it was, and they were, therefore, comfortable with one another.

There was a knock at the door, and Laura got up to answer it. She stood in the doorway, opening the door only partially.

"Oh, it's you," she said. "What do you want?"

Henry could not see the man in the hallway, but he could hear the voice.

"I want to talk to you," it said.

"We've got nothing to talk about," said Laura. "Just leave me alone."

"Let me come in," said the man.

"No."

"Just for a minute."

"The last time I let you in just for a minute, we wound up in a hell of a fight, and you blacked my eye," said Laura. "Just go away and leave me alone."

"Laura," said the man, and he pushed on the door.

Henry stood up from his place on the couch, and his eyes caught the eyes of the man in the hall for an instant. Then the other stepped back and disappeared from Henry's view once more.

"I didn't know you had company," said the voice.

"You didn't need to know," said Laura. "Now go away and don't come back."

She slammed the door, turned around and leaned against it with an exasperated sigh.

"I'm sorry about that," she said.

"Who is he?" asked Henry.

"My ex-husband. He keeps bothering me. Says he wants me back. Let's not talk about him, okay?"

Henry sat back down. The existence of the ex-husband didn't worry him. If need be, he could take care of the man. But the fact that Laura had something even more to escape than the general dreariness of life in Pueblo helped Henry to make a quick decision on a matter he had been contemplating since he had read his latest mail.

"I'm going back to Oklahoma, Laura," he said. "I want you to go with me."

"What?" she said, moving back to the couch to sit beside him.

"You heard me."

"Wait a minute, baby," said Laura. "There's a couple of problems with that idea."

"What's wrong with it?" said Henry.

"If you leave the state, you violate your parole. They'll send you back to prison."

Henry stood up and paced across the room.

"If I can't move when I feel like it," he said, "I might as well be in prison anyway. I'm going. I'll change my name, and I'll live in Tulsa. It's getting big enough that I can hide there."

"All right," said Laura. "Then the other thing. You want me to go with you?"

"That's right," said Henry. "That's what I said."

"What about your wife in Tulsa?"

Henry clenched his jaws slightly, then relaxed. He reached into a pocket of his jacket, which was hanging on the back of a chair, and withdrew a folded-up piece of paper. He handed the paper to Laura, who opened it up to read.

"This is a letter from your wife?" she said.

"Uh-huh."

"She's gotten a divorce."

Laura refolded the letter and handed it back to Henry.

"So I'm a free man," he said with a grin, "uh, so to speak."

32

It was good to be back in Oklahoma, changed though it was. Henry had come to expect change—radical change—every time he returned home. Change comes gradually to those who remain at home, and, more often than not, they take it in stride—don't even notice it creeping up on them. Henry, having spent long periods of time away from home, always saw the changes when he returned, and each time he returned to that place he called home and found it again strange to him, he felt more isolated—estranged from not only society but also the landscape. He was the stranger. No matter where he might go, he would always be a stranger. He had accepted that role as a permanent fixture of his life on this planet, as a part of the hand he had been dealt by a cold and impersonal fate.

He went back to Tulsa, a fugitive from the state of Colorado, bringing the white woman, Laura, with him. They went into Tulsa as man and wife, using the names of Mr. and Mrs. R. L. Williamson. Henry enjoyed taking Laura to a Tulsa realtor and being shown houses. He particularly enjoyed the fact that Mr. and Mrs. Williamson finally settled for a modest home two doors down from the home of the sheriff of Tulsa County. It was 1914, and Henry Starr was forty-one years old. He found a publisher, R. D. Gordon, in Tulsa, who was willing to bring out his book. Gordon was unaware of Henry's life as R. L. Williamson and had no address for Henry. The book was published that same year under the title, *Thrilling Events: Life of Henry Starr, Written in the Colorado Penitentiary by*

Himself. It sold for fifty cents, and it sold fairly well. It was 1914, the year of the assassination of Archduke Ferdinand and the beginning of World War I. It was the year that William S. Hart starred in his first Western film, *The Bargain.* And it was the year that, beginning on September 8, in Keystone, Oklahoma, and ending on December 29, in Carney, Kansas, nine banks were robbed, and Henry Starr was said to have robbed them all. He had no job, either as Henry Starr or as R. L. Williamson, and his earnings from *Thrilling Events* were scant.

It was also an election year in Oklahoma. The governor was named R. L. Williams. Reading the paper in his modest little house, Henry Starr chuckled at the nearness of his assumed name to that of the governor. Then he came across another interesting bit of news.

"Ha," he said. "Laura. Listen to this. Al Jennings, the old train robber, is a candidate for the office of governor."

"A train robber," said Laura, "running for governor? Is he crazy?"

"No," said Henry, "actually I think he should win the office. He's a better man than the average politician, for he has at least been open and honest about his stealing."

"Well," said Laura.

"And furthermore," continued Henry, "he has already served his time in prison for his previous crimes, which is more than any of the others can say."

Henry's sense of humor often eluded Laura, and this was one of those times. She shrugged and went on about her business, while Henry continued reading the paper.

"It says here," said Henry, "that the leading candidate is by far the incumbent, Governor R. L. Williams."

"Huh," said Laura, who had never before noticed the name, "that sounds almost like you—R. L. Williamson."

"Yes."

Henry had lowered the paper. He was deep in thought. "I wonder what would happen if I, Mr. R. L. Williamson, should file for office. I wonder how many voters might become confused and cast for me by mistake."

The following morning Henry kissed Laura good-bye, went downtown, and filed for office under his assumed name. He went from there to the train station and caught a train for Webster Groves, Missouri. There he robbed the bank and caught the next train back to Tulsa.

The year 1915 began with the incumbent having been elected for another term as governor of the state. Henry's game had, indeed, drawn some votes away from the governor, but not enough to cost him the election. The year also began with a new string of bank robberies, all attributed to Henry Starr. In January alone, the banks were robbed in Preston, Owasso, Terlton, Garber, and Vera. Governor Williams authorized a thousand-dollar reward for the capture of Henry Starr—dead or alive. Henry wrote a letter to the governor.

33

Governor R. L. Williams roared up out of the giant plush office chair in which he sat behind the vast, uncluttered desk in his office in the new state capitol at Oklahoma City. The man standing before the desk quivered back out of the way.

"Miss Crump," called the governor, "fetch me the damned letter from the file."

Miss Crump, who had been standing dutifully beside the door just inside the governor's office, came to attention.

"Yes, sir," she said, and scurried out the door.

"George," said the governor, "get out and find Nix and get him back here to my office damned quick."

"Yes, sir," said George, turning briskly and following Miss Crump out the door.

All this while, a second man had been standing quietly aside against one wall. With everyone else out of the way, the governor turned on him.

"Andy," he said, "we've got to straighten this mess out damned fast, or I may be made to look like a damned fool."

"Yes, sir," said Andy. "If I could just get a look at the . . ."

Just then Miss Crump came briskly back into the room. Her words cut Andy off in the middle of his sentence.

"Here's the letter, Governor," she said.

". . . the letter, yes," said Andy, valiantly concluding his rudely interrupted statement.

The governor, red-faced and sweating, snatched the letter from Miss Crump's hand.

"Give it to me," he said. "Here. Listen to this, Andy. Just listen, and then tell me what the hell we're going to do. Listen."

Williams adjusted a pair of glasses on the end of his nose and carefully positioned the letter before him. Then he started reading aloud.

" 'Governor,' it says, 'what does the legislature and also you mean by having a reward of a thousand dollars for me, dead or alive, for robbing banks? Now, Governor, I did not know this reward was out for me, for I have not been in Oklahoma for three years or more, and I can prove it by fifty men here in Reno.

" 'Now, Governor, you surely cannot have a reward for me for a thing I did not do, and you have been misled as to me having been in any of these bank robberies. Sam Cook says . . .' "

Here the governor stopped reading and looked up over the letter and his glasses.

"Who the hell is Sam Cook, Andy?" he said.

"I don't know, sir."

" 'Sam Cook,' " the governor continued, " 'says you are a fair and square man. You will do square with anyone, and after you have found that you have been misled, I hope you will be fair with me. I suppose I will be accused all my life, no matter if I am in Australia. Yours respectfully, Henry Starr.' "

Williams lowered the letter and removed his glasses. He glared at Andy for a moment.

"Did you listen, Andy?" he asked. "Did you hear all that?"

"Yes, sir," said Andy. "May I please see the letter?"

"Huh? Oh, yes," said the governor, a bit absentmindedly. "Here it is."

He handed the letter to Andy, who began reading it for

himself. The governor seemed momentarily lost in his own thoughts.

"It's a respectful letter, Andy," he said. "It's respectful of my position."

Andy still perused the letter. He made no response to the governor.

"The man has been wrongfully accused in the past," said the governor. "That's what made him a criminal in the first place. It says so right here."

He rushed around his desk and picked up a copy of *Thrilling Events*, waving it out before him at Andy to emphasize his point.

"Now, what if he is innocent of these robberies, and we're guilty of repeating the same old pattern? Andy, that would make me look just awful."

Andy was still lost in the letter and did not answer, but before the governor could say anything more, George came back into the office, followed by a large man of about fifty, wearing tall black boots, dusty trail clothes, and a badge, and carrying a wide-brimmed hat.

"Nix," the governor shouted, rushing toward the big man, "come in. Come in. We've got to straighten this mess out. We've done gone and accused Henry Starr of robbing all these banks and damned if he ain't way out there in Reno, Nevada, and been there for three years. And we've put a price on his head. A thousand dollars, Nix, a thousand dollars."

Nix was calm. His demeanor bespoke confidence, and when he spoke, his voice was low and smooth.

"How do we know he's in Reno?" he asked.

Andy stepped toward Nix, holding out the letter.

"Well," he said, "here's the letter the governor received from the Hotel Reno signed by Henry Starr."

"Let me see," said Nix, taking the letter from Andy.

"What the hell are we going to do?" shouted the governor. "We've got to do something right away. Nix?"

Miss Crump had stepped back inside the office and was edging her way timidly toward the men, who stood in a cluster in the center of the office. She wanted to interrupt them, but she was obviously a lady who knew her place. Nix scratched his chin.

"Hmm," he muttered. "If this is true, we've made a serious error."

"We can't let my political opponents get ahold of this," said the governor. "And the press. George, the press. You've got to handle the press on this matter, George."

"We just have to check this out," said Andy. "What if we write a letter to the Hotel Reno?"

"Write, hell," shouted the governor. "I'm sending Nix up there."

"Governor," said Miss Crump tentatively.

"Not now, Miss Crump."

"We need to know just exactly who, in each case," said Nix, "accused Starr of the recent robberies—and on what basis."

The governor began pacing furiously back and forth across his office floor.

"We need to know if there's really fifty men in Reno," he said, "who'll swear he's been there for three years."

Miss Crump gathered all her strength of will and stepped in front of Williams, bringing his pacing to an abrupt halt. She thrust an envelope in front of his face.

"Governor, excuse me," she said, "but will this help?"

"No, Miss Crump," said the governor impatiently. "Not now."

"Wait," said Nix. "Wait a minute. What is that?"

"It's the envelope the letter came in," said Miss Crump.

Nix snatched it from Miss Crump and looked it over hurriedly.

"Let me see it," he said. "It's Hotel Reno, all right."

"Excuse me, Mr. Nix," said Miss Crump, "but—the postmark."

"What?"

"The postmark."

"Oh, yes," said Nix, "the postmark."

"It's postmarked right up in Tulsa," said Miss Crump. "Well? Does that help?"

34

Henry Starr sat at the head of the dining table in his Tulsa home. Around the table sat Lewis Estes, Bud Maxfield, Claud Sawyer, Al Spencer, and Grover Durrell—all white men. They were men Henry Starr had carefully searched for. All were known and wanted criminals. The hardcases listened intently as Henry talked.

"The reason I've gotten all of you together," he said, "is to make bank robbing history. I've already robbed more banks than any man in history, at least, that's what they're saying about me, so robbing just one more won't make a whole lot of difference to me. But no one has yet succeeded at robbing two banks at one time."

Estes' eyes opened wide.

"Two banks at one time?" he said.

There were murmurs around the table. Henry paused to allow the rumbling to subside on its own. When the men around the table were quiet again, he went on.

"The Dalton boys tried it in Coffeyville back in '92 and got wiped out in the attempt. Here it is 1915. That was twenty-three years ago, and no one's done it yet. But we're going to do it, and do it right."

"Where at?" said Spencer.

Henry looked over the faces around the table. The men were all quiet, all watching him and waiting for his answer. If there had been initial objections, they had seemingly vanished.

"Stroud, Oklahoma," he said.

On March 27, 1915, on the main street of Stroud, Bud

Maxfield stood with six horses at a hitch rail in front of a store. A few doors down from where Maxfield waited, Henry Starr, Estes, and Sawyer opened the front door of a bank and walked in. Out in the middle of the street, just as the third man disappeared into the bank, Spencer and Durrell pulled out their pistols and fired a few shots into the air. The shots had the desired effect. People on the street ran inside of doors—whatever doors were handy. The street was cleared. One of those who ran for cover was sixteen-year-old Paul Curry. He ducked inside a butcher shop that stood between the bank and the store-front where Maxfield waited with the horses. Spencer and Durrell, holding their guns ready for action, kept turning to look from one end of the street to the other, watching nervously for any sign of interference with their plans. A door opened next door to the bank, and Spencer whirled to level his six-shooter at whoever might come out. Who-ever it was saw Spencer and immediately reconsidered. The door shut again quickly. Then Henry, Estes, and Sawyer came back out of the bank, each with money sacks stuffed. They calmly walked into the street, heading for the second bank, just across from the first one. In the middle of the street Spencer and Durrell turned and fell in step with the other three, and all five walked into the second bank.

Across the street in the butcher shop, young Paul Curry watched, fascinated, through a dirty window in the front door. His heart pounded, and he felt his breath heavy in his chest. He saw the five men come back out of the bank across the street from him. Each man carried a sack stuffed, apparently, with cash. The five men were walking across the street at an angle that would take them directly to the six horses and the sixth man who waited for them. Young Curry realized that the bank robbers would have to walk right past the butcher shop—right past him.

"No one's doing anything," he said to himself.

The robbers were almost in front of him.

"They're just walking away from the bank. No one's making a move."

Paul looked around frantically inside the shop. There in a corner was an old rifle the butcher used for killing hogs. Paul ran to it and grabbed it up. He checked nervously to see if it was loaded. It was. He stepped back to the door. The outlaws had passed the butcher shop and were almost to their horses.

Out in the street Henry took up the rear in the move back to the horses. He felt, as always, something like a military commander with the responsibility for the safety of his command on his shoulders. He would be the last one to mount up and ride away. Moving at an easy pace, he spoke to his gang.

"Well, boys," he said, "we've accomplished a bank robber's dream and outdone the Daltons all at once. Now let's mount up and see if we can get out of here in one piece."

Estes snorted over his shoulder.

"Hell," he said, "ain't no one trying to stop us."

As Spencer and Durrell, the first to reach the horses, were climbing into their saddles, Paul Curry opened the front door of the butcher shop. Rifle in hand, he stepped out into the street. He put the hog-killing rifle to his shoulder, aimed, and fired. Henry Starr felt the slap against his hip an instant before he heard the report of the rifle. His legs quit working, and he crumpled into the dirt. The other five hesitated, confused. Henry called out to them from where he lay in the street.

"Go on, boys," he said. "Get out of here."

The five outlaws put their spurs to their mounts and rode quickly out of Stroud, and Henry Starr lay looking into the tough faces of a crowd of armed and irate citizens that had suddenly materialized around him. They had found their bravery, he thought, after he had fallen wounded and the others had ridden off. He glanced back toward the butcher shop where he knew the shot had come from, and he saw the young Paul Curry with the hog rifle. Not only that, his thought continued, they had let a kid do the only shooting of the day for them. He lay back in the dirt street and relaxed to await his fate.

35

Henry Starr was sentenced to twenty-five years in the Oklahoma State Penitentiary at McAlester. He was forty-three years old. It was the year that Henry James died, and the United States Supreme Court decided that an Indian could still be treated as a ward of the United States Government and Congress could still regulate his affairs for him. During Henry's second year at McAlester, William C. Rogers, the current nominal Principal Chief of the Cherokee Nation, died, and the Bolshevik Revolution occurred in Russia. In Henry's third year at McAlester, Redbird Smith, the Chief of the Nighthawk Keetoowahs, died, and World War I came to an end. During his fourth year, he was granted a parole, having been, as before, a model prisoner and well liked by all.

Henry was in his cell waiting. He had already received word that his parole had been granted and in a few days he would be released. He tried to imagine what it would be like to be on the outside again. He had discovered that during these long prison stays, prison life came to seem to be normal life. Life on the outside seemed unreal.

Footsteps interrupted Henry's thoughts. A guard came walking down the hall with a man Henry had not seen before. They stopped at Henry's cell. Henry stood up from where he had been lying on the cot.

"Hello, Henry," said the guard.

"Hello, Marvin."

"Henry, this is Cooper Neal. He's a reporter from

Oklahoma City. He'd like to talk to you. The warden okayed it, if it's all right with you."

"Hello, Mr. Starr," said Neal.

"Mr. Neal," said Henry. "Sure, Marvin. It's okay."

Marvin unlocked the cell door to let Neal inside with Henry. He locked it again behind Neal.

"I'll be back in a bit," he said, then walked off down the hallway.

Henry gestured toward the cot.

"It's all I've got to offer," he said. "Sit down."

"Thank you," said Neal, removing a pad and pencil from his coat pocket and sitting on the edge of the cot. "Do you mind if I take notes?"

"Not at all."

Henry sat down at the other end of the cot.

"To what do I owe this visit?" he said.

"Mr. Starr," said Neal, "you're a famous man. You successfully engineered the robbing of two banks at Stroud. Even the Dalton Gang failed to pull off that kind of a job."

"But I didn't walk away from it," said Henry.

"Even before that job, you had robbed more banks than any man in history."

"That's what they tell me, although I've been given credit for some that I didn't do."

"Mr. Starr, you wrote your life story while you were in prison in Colorado. That's been a few years ago now. Will you work some more on that to bring it up to date?"

"No," said Henry, "I doubt that I'll return to that task. I'll leave it to someone else to put the finish to it—if anyone's interested."

Neal scribbled hasty notes.

"Well," he said, "uh, you've had the experience of several prisons now. How do you feel about this one here at McAlester?"

Henry chuckled and leaned back against the cell wall. He crossed his hands behind his head.

"At least I won't have far to travel to get back home when I finally get out of here," he said, but having said it, he asked himself where his home might be. Oklahoma was home. Beyond that, he couldn't say. He couldn't get any closer to it than that.

"Yes," said Neal, still scribbling. "You were in Ohio and in Colorado, weren't you?"

"That's right."

"How do they compare?"

"I believe that they'd all do a better job," said Henry, suddenly serious, "if they adopted Warden Tynan's honor system."

"Warden Tynan?"

"He's the warden at Canyon City."

"That's Colorado?"

"He was first ridiculed and sneered at," said Henry, "but his honor system is a success, and even those who knocked it now have to admit that the warden knew what he was doing. Now seven other states that I know of have adopted it, but not, unfortunately, Oklahoma. I don't think that they'll keep me in here any longer for having said that."

"Um, I see," said Neal. "Well, now, Mr. Starr, I have just a few more quick questions to ask, if you don't mind."

"Shoot."

"What are your politics?" asked Neal.

"Haven't any."

"Your religion?"

"Same."

"Do you think that you have led a correct life?"

"No, but it's as good as some others that are holding office."

"Don't you think that it's a great crime to take people's money?"

"Yes. I know it's wrong, but I am only a small thief. The lawyers take it all away from me, and still I go to the penitentiary. The big thieves never go to the pen, and they keep what they steal. For that reason, I feel much abused."

Neal paused and cleared his throat.

"You, of course," he said, "are an Indian."

"I have never," said Henry, "been mistaken for a Swede."

"Uh, yes. Uh, what do you think about the treatment your people have received?"

Henry looked Neal in the eyes, and Neal, try as he might, couldn't break loose from that gaze to return to his notes.

"If we believe in the law of compensation," said Henry, "then the white folks of these United States are sure in for some bad luck. If not, why, then, the meanest and strongest get the biggest loaf, with no fixed or immutable laws, but a haphazard conglomeration that is liable to skid into oblivion."

Neal went back to Oklahoma City and wrote his story. His editor was pleased. Neal also reread his copy of *Thrilling Events*, and he never got over the effects of his interview with Henry Starr.

On March 15, 1919, Henry Starr, dressed in a new civilian suit, stood at the front gate of the Oklahoma State Penitentiary. He handed a piece of paper to the gate guard.

"Well, Henry," said the guard, "you going home?"

"I'm not exactly sure where that is anymore, Gerald," said Henry.

Gerald opened the gate for Henry to walk through, then shut it again and locked it. Henry stood on the outside of the gate looking ahead.

"Hey," said Gerald, through the gate, "how much time have you done?"

"Altogether?"

"Yeah."

"Just over fifteen years," said Henry.

"You got early outs, too, didn't you?"

"For good behavior."

"What if you hadn't?" said the guard. "I mean, how much time would it have been?"

"I've been sentenced to a total of sixty-five years in prison—that's not to mention the time I was sentenced to hang."

Gerald shook his head.

"Hmm," he murmured. "Well, I'll be seeing you."

"No," said Henry. "No, you won't. So long."

36

On the main street of Stroud, Oklahoma, a man stood with six horses at a hitch rail in front of a store. A few doors down from where he waited, Henry Starr and two other men opened the front door of a bank and walked in. Out in the middle of the street, just as the third man disappeared into the bank, two men pulled out their pistols and fired a few shots into the air. The shots had the desired effect. People on the street ran inside of doors— whatever doors were handy. The street was cleared. One of those who ran for cover was a sixteen-year-old boy. He ducked inside a butcher shop that stood between the bank and the storefront where the man waited with the horses. The two men in the middle of the street, holding their guns ready for action, kept turning to look from one end of the street to the other, watching nervously for any sign of interference with their plans. A door opened next door to the bank, and one of the men whirled to level his six-shooter at whoever might come out. Whoever it was saw him and immediately reconsidered. The door shut again quickly. Then Henry and the two men with him came back out of the bank, each with money sacks stuffed. They calmly walked into the street, heading for the second bank, just across from the first one. In the middle of the street, the two men stationed there turned and fell in step with the other three, and all five walked into the second bank.

Across the street in the butcher shop, the young man

watched, fascinated, through a dirty window in the front door. His heart pounded, and he felt his breath heavy in his chest. He saw the five men come out of the bank across the street from him. Each man carried a sack stuffed, apparently, with cash. The five men were walking across the street at an angle that would take them directly to the six horses and the sixth man who waited for them. The young man in the butcher shop realized that the bank robbers would have to walk right past the butcher shop—right past him.

"No one's doing anything," he said.

The robbers were almost in front of him.

"They're just walking away from the bank. No one's making a move."

He looked around frantically inside the shop. There in a corner was an old rifle the butcher used for killing hogs. He ran to it and grabbed it up. He checked nervously to see if it was loaded. It was. He stepped back to the door. The outlaws had passed the butcher shop and were almost to their horses.

Out in the street, Henry took up the rear in the move back to the horses. He felt, as always, something like a military commander with the responsibility for the safety of his command on his shoulders. He would be the last one to mount up and ride away. Moving at an easy pace, he spoke to his gang.

"Well, boys," he said, "we've accomplished a bank robber's dream and outdone the Daltons all at once. Now let's mount up and see if we can get out of here in one piece."

One of the men snorted over his shoulder.

"Hell," he said, "ain't no one trying to stop us."

As the first two men reached their horses and were climbing into their saddles, the young man opened the front door of the butcher shop. Rifle in hand, he stepped out into the street. He put the hog-killing rifle to his shoulder, aimed, and fired. Henry Starr's legs gave out under him, and he crumpled into the dirt. The other five hesitated, confused. Henry called out to them from where he lay in the street.

"Go on, boys," he said. "Get out of here."

The five outlaws put their spurs to their mounts and rode quickly out of Stroud, and Henry Starr lay looking into the tough faces of a crowd of armed and irate citizens that had suddenly materialized around him.

"Cut. Cut."

The five riders had halted their mounts at the end of the street, and when they heard the shout, they turned and loped them back to the spot from which they had started. The young man laid aside the hog-gun and sat down on the edge of the sidewalk. A balding, middle-aged man in a beret, a flower-printed short-sleeved shirt, and knickers, holding a megaphone in his right hand, stepped out into the street. All eyes were turned in his direction.

"That's a take," he said. "Henry, baby, that was fantastic."

Henry stood up and dusted off his clothes the best he could. The man with the megaphone continued talking.

"All right, everyone," he said, "let's wrap it up for the day. Be back at the studio in the morning at eight o'clock sharp. Sharp, now."

He stepped over to another man who stood behind a massive camera on a tripod and slapped him on the shoulder. Henry walked past them to a white woman who waited there in a spot on the sidewalk out of the way. She was probably crowding forty, but she was carefully made up and fashionably dressed. She was an attractive woman —one who obviously knew just how attractive she was and was working hard to maintain that attractiveness in the wake of the ravages of age. He put an arm around her shoulder and squeezed her affectionately. She kissed him on the cheek.

"You were wonderful, darling," she said.

"It was easy," said Henry. "It didn't hurt nearly as much as the first time."

The woman's name was Lillian. She had more or less come with the film deal; at least, she had dropped into Henry's life at about that same time. Henry couldn't even recall just when and where he had first seen her. It didn't really matter, anyway. If she had not been there, another would have been. Lillian, Laura, Mae—what did it matter? But then there had been Olive—Olive and little Theodore Roosevelt Starr. Henry tried not to think of them. There were always people around him—men and women —and he was always alone.

They dined together, Henry and Lillian, at a fine new restaurant in downtown Tulsa, and then they walked to the new movie theater. The streets were busy with automobiles, the air filled with the sounds of their engines and of honking horns and of the odor of exhaust fumes. In front of the theater stood a life-sized cardboard cutout of Henry Starr, wearing tall black boots, his trousers tucked into them. He had on a white Stetson, and around his neck was tied a large yellow bandanna. He held a six-gun in each hand and glared menacingly straight ahead. The real Henry Starr stepped up beside the copy and struck a similar pose. He wore a new western suit, boots, string tie, and white Stetson. Lillian laughed, a lilting, musical laugh, at his posture. Crowds of moviegoers pointed and whispered to each other. Behind the two figures of Henry Starr, on the front of the theater building was pasted a poster advertising the movie inside: *"A Debtor to the Law,* starring Henry Starr, the notorious bank robber, as himself."

Inside, Henry sat with the white woman in darkness in the midst of a crowd. He held her hand. Their eyes, like those of the rest of the crowd, stared straight ahead at flickering images on a large screen. The movements of the figures on the screen were strange, jerky, a little comical, but Henry was recognizable as one of the six men on horseback riding into town. The town, too, was recognizable to anyone who had been there. It was Stroud, Oklahoma.

It was strange for Henry, watching himself rob the two banks at Stroud. He saw the horses hitched to the rail in front of the store. He watched himself walking down the street and into the first bank. He saw the two men in the street, and he saw the boy go into the butcher shop. The reenactment was accurate, precise. Henry had insisted that it be so. The only thing unreal to Henry was that the faces of his cohorts were not those of Estes, Maxfield, Sawyer, Spencer, and Durrell. They were, instead, faces of actors. And, of course, there was no sound other than that of the rinky-tink piano off to the left of the screen. It was, to Henry, like a dream. It was surreal. It was as if he were there again, going through it all again, yet he wasn't, and when the young actor playing the part of Paul Curry fired the shot that dropped Henry in the street, Henry flinched in his chair and a sharp pain shot through his hip.

The movie ended, and the house lights were turned on, temporarily blinding everyone in the audience, and Henry and Lillian strolled out into the street. He was easily recognized. Some groups of people, as had those before the start of the movie, whispered and pointed. Others spoke to him and shook his hand. He signed some autographs, some on small picture postcards bearing his image. When he finally managed to break away from his fans, Henry walked his woman back to their hotel. On the way through the lobby, the desk clerk called out.

"Mr. Starr."

Henry turned to face the man.

"Yeah?"

"I have a letter for you here, sir. Just delivered."

Henry walked over to the counter and got the letter. He studied the return address and the postmark on the envelope.

"What is it?" said Lillian.

"From those Hollywood people," said Henry. "Let's go upstairs."

They went to their room, and Henry tossed his hat onto a chair. He tore open the envelope and read the letter.

"Well?" said Lillian.

"This California company wants me to go out there and go to work for them staging bank robberies for their western movies."

"Oh," said Lillian, "that sounds wonderful. You will go, won't you?"

"I don't know," said Henry. "I'm thinking about it. I've made three movies for this other outfit, and I'm broke. I don't even have the cash to pay our way out of this room."

"But this will pay well," said Lillian. "Real well."

"It's a sad comment on society," said Henry, "that when a bank robber tries to reform, the people he works for will rob him blind. These movie people are worse crooks than I ever was. Still, the only other trade I have that pays well is bank robbing. We'll need some cash to make the move."

The big touring car sped down the narrow and winding Arkansas blacktop road leading into the bustling town of Harrison. Two men in business suits rode in the front, Henry Starr sat in the back alone. Tires squealed as the automobile took a sharp curve too quickly and started on the downhill grade with the outskirts of Harrison at its base. From the back seat Henry punched the driver in the shoulder and called out to him in a loud voice calculated to compensate for the roar of the wind and of the engine and of the loud whine of the tires on the blacktop.

"Slow this thing down," he said. "We don't want to call attention to ourselves on the way in."

The driver did slow down, and the car rolled into Harrison drawing only incidental attention. He pulled up and parked in front of the bank on the main street and set the hand brake. The three men got out and walked to the front door of the bank. At a nod from Henry, the other two men reached under their suit coats and pulled out handguns. One of them opened the door and stepped aside, as Henry vaulted into the bank lobby, a pistol in each hand.

"Hands up and hands steady," he called out.

His two companions were inside just after him, both holding their pistols out in front of them. There were few customers in the bank, and none of them panicked. They stepped back and put their hands up as they had been ordered to do. One of Henry's companions held his pistol on the customers. The other moved quickly to behind the counter and began gathering cash up from the several cashiers' drawers. Henry walked up to the window where a man stood with his hands up. The name plate in front of him said, "William J. Myers." The big bank vault was behind Myers. Myers eyed Henry's revolver nervously.

"Mr. Myers," said Henry, "open that vault."

Myers turned slowly and deliberately and stepped to the vault. The vault was not locked, for all he did was turn the handle and pull open the heavy door. It was a large walk-in vault, and Henry's intention was to go inside and clean it out. He put a hand on Myers' back and gave him a persuasive shove.

"Inside," he said.

Myers went into the vault, and Henry looked over his shoulder to check on his two cohorts before following Myers into the vault himself. In that instant Myers, inside the vault, reached into a corner and picked up a double-barreled shotgun that had been stashed there for just such an emergency. Henry turned to walk into the vault and looked into the two big barrels. He didn't have time to react. Myers pulled the triggers, and the roar filled the bank. The tremendous impact of the shot at such close range blew Henry back against the counter.

It was 1921. Henry Starr was forty-seven years old, and he was dying in Harrison, Arkansas, following an attempt to rob the bank there. His two unknown companions had escaped with the money they had taken from the cashiers' drawers. They did not get the money out of the vault, for when Henry had been shot, they had immediately fled the scene. Woodrow Wilson was President of the United States. The League of Nations had been established, and the United States Congress had passed the Nineteenth Amendment to the United States Constitution, granting women the right to vote. Tom Mix starred in eight Western movies that year, and, that year, Gooper Johnson would perform the service for which he had been paid several years previous and bury Henry Starr in Dewey, Oklahoma. The twenty-nine-year career of outlawry had come to an end. Henry regained consciousness lying in what he knew would be his deathbed there in a cell in the Harrison jail. Johnson would earn the fee he had paid him for the funeral. He was confident of that. A doctor had seen him and treated him. He could tell. He was bandaged. He felt no pain. He felt tired—numb. When they discovered that he was conscious, a small crowd came into the cell and gathered around his cot—his deathbed. A photographer took his picture lying there. Henry didn't care. He had seen photographs of the dead bodies of the Daltons taken at Coffeyville and of Ned Christie's body roped to a slab and displayed in Arkansas. At least Henry was still alive. Someone spoke to him. He couldn't tell who it was. The voice was faint and faraway sounding, but he did understand the question.

"Henry, do you have anything to say?"

It took all his strength and will, but Henry was determined to answer. He did have something to say, something he wanted everyone to hear, something for the reporters to write about, something for all the world to read. It didn't matter who was there in the cell in the small crowd. It didn't matter who it might be who had asked the question. He would give them his answer and someone would repeat it. It would be heard.

"I've robbed more banks than any man in history," he said.

And that was the end. He died as he had lived—alone and in a crowd.

About the Author

Robert J. Conley is a Western writer and editor who specializes in Cherokee lore. He is a former Professor of Indian Studies and English. He is currently living in Tahlequah, Oklahoma, and is the author of two previous Double D Westerns, *Back to Malachi* and *The Actor*.